CLUB

CSI:™

The Case of the Mystery Meat Loaf

by David Lewman

Simon Spotlight

New York   London   Toronto   Sydney   New Delhi

SIMON SPOTLIGHT

An imprint of Simon & Schuster Children's Publishing Division
1230 Avenue of the Americas, New York, New York 10020
© 2012 by CBS Broadcasting Inc. and Entertainment AB Funding LLC.
All Rights Reserved. CSI: CRIME SCENE INVESTIGATION in USA is a trademark of CBS Broadcasting Inc. and outside USA is a trademark of Entertainment AB Funding LLC.
All rights reserved, including the right of reproduction in whole or in part in any form. SIMON SPOTLIGHT and colophon are registered trademarks of Simon & Schuster, Inc. For information about special discounts for bulk purchases, please contact Simon & Schuster Special Sales at 1-866-506-1949 or business@simonandschuster.com.
Manufactured in the United States of America 0312 FFG
First Edition 10 9 8 7 6 5 4 3 2 1
ISBN 978-1-4424-4646-5 (hc)
ISBN 978-1-4424-3394-6 (pbk)
Library of Congress Catalog Card Number 2011934860

Cover illustration by Chris King
Design by Victor Joseph Ochoa

Hannah, Ben, and Corey hurried down the long hallway of Woodlands Junior High. The three best friends didn't want to be late for their first class with Mr. Longfellow, the earth science teacher.

"I hear he's really strict," Hannah said, worried.

"And old," Ben added, nodding.

"I hear he knows so much about rocks because he was there when they made 'em," Corey said. All three laughed.

As they climbed the stairs to the second floor, Hannah asked, "So, what'd you do over break?"

Corey grinned. "Video games and basketball. Working on my dunk."

Hannah looked skeptical. "You can dunk?"

"In the video game, yeah," Corey answered. "What'd you do?"

Hannah shifted her backpack to her other shoulder. "Well, practicing for my ballet recital took a lot of time."

"You were a mouse, right?" Corey asked, smiling.

Hannah rolled her eyes and then laughed. "I haven't been a mouse in years! I was a snowflake. And that was in *The Nutcracker*, back in December. This was a regular recital with my ballet class."

"Promotion—nice." Corey turned to Ben. "And how did you spend your vacation?"

Ben blinked and looked a little embarrassed. "I thought since we were going to start a new class in earth science, it might be interesting to read a book about geology. . . ."

"You spent spring break studying?" Hannah asked incredulously.

"And you find that surprising because . . . ?" Corey asked, laughing.

"What?" Ben protested. "It wasn't an assigned book, so technically I wasn't studying!"

The bell rang just as Hannah touched the door to the science lab. "And technically we're on time," she said.

She opened the door, and they slipped into the lab, which smelled like chemicals. After they found three seats together, they noticed a slim young woman standing at the front of the class. Her dark hair was pulled into a messy bun at the nape of her neck, with a pencil stuck through it. She wore a loose-fitting black dress with a cropped jean jacket—and cowboy boots. Hannah, who had never thought cowboy boots could look so good with a dress, thought she looked totally cool.

Corey whispered, "Mr. Longfellow looks nothing like I pictured him."

As Hannah suppressed a giggle, the woman set a cardboard box on the desk and began to speak. "Good morning, class. My name is Miss Hodges. I know you were expecting Mr. Longfellow to teach earth science, but there's been a change of plans."

She turned to the dry-erase board and wrote her name. "Mr. Longfellow has retired. So you're stuck with me." She smiled.

Hannah, Ben, and Corey exchanged quick looks. From everything they'd heard about Mr. Longfellow, Miss Hodges was going to be a big improvement. She was young! She dressed cool! She smiled!

The new semester was looking better already!

"And even though this is still a science class," she continued, "the curriculum has been changed to match my specialty." As she spoke, Miss Hodges wrote "Forensic Science" on the board in clear, bold letters and then underlined it. "Who can tell me what this means?"

Ben raised his hand, and Miss Hodges nodded toward him. "'Forensic' has to do with legal arguing or debating. So 'forensic science' is coming up with evidence to support your argument, usually in court."

Miss Hodges nodded, impressed. "Very good! This semester we're going to learn about the science of gathering and evaluating evidence."

Some of the students looked intrigued. Others looked a little thrown. They'd been expecting a class in earth science, but now it sounded as though they were going to learn how to become detectives or something. This obviously wasn't going to be your average science class.

Miss Hodges continued, "My cousin works in a crime lab in Las Vegas, so we may even get the opportunity to—"

Just then the door to the room burst open. A figure dashed in, snatched the box off Miss Hodges's desk, yelled something, and ran back out of the lab. A couple of students quickly stood up, and a few frantically dug out their phones.

Miss Hodges raised her hands, motioning for everyone to sit down. "Put your phones away. Everything's okay. Please take out a piece of paper and write down a short description of what just happened. Don't discuss it, just write down a description of what you saw."

Puzzled, the students sat down, pulled paper out of their backpacks, and started writing. Miss Hodges walked around the room, quietly observing what the students were writing. She nodded and raised her eyebrows as she observed. After a few minutes she asked them to stop by saying, "Okay, pencils down!"

"Now," she said, sitting on the edge of her desk instead of behind it. "Be honest. How many of you wrote that the person who ran in here was wearing a hat?"

Only about eight students raised their hands. "What color was the hat?" Miss Hodges asked. Corey raised his hand. "Yes?"

"Black. He wore a black hat," Corey answered confidently.

"Dude, his hat was brown," Ricky Collins argued from the back of the room. Ricky was a big tough kid whose mom ran the school cafeteria.

"I'm pretty sure it was blue," a shy girl named Katie said quietly. "Also, it wasn't a guy. It was a girl."

The students started to argue about what they'd seen. Miss Hodges listened for a few moments and then raised her hands for quiet. "So what did the person yell?" she asked, bringing the room back to order.

They all had different opinions about that, too. Some thought the intruder had yelled, "This is mine!" Others were sure he (or she) had shouted, "Free your mind!" One girl even thought the thief had said, "Kisses are fine!" but she was in a minority of one.

Miss Hodges laughed. "Let's find out, shall we?" She opened the door to the lab and leaned into the hall. "Come on back in," she called.

A short girl dressed in black came into the class. She was carrying the box and wearing a brown knit hat. "See? Brown hat!" Ricky said, gloating.

6

"True, but she's a girl," Hannah pointed out.

"Yeah, I noticed," said Ricky. A couple of boys laughed.

"Thank you, Stephanie," Miss Hodges said to the girl. "Good job." The girl smiled, set down the box, and started to leave. "Oh, by the way," Miss Hodges added. "What did you yell when you came in here?"

Stephanie giggled. "It was gibberish—'Gisha nine.' Just like you told me to say." Giving a little good-bye wave to the class, she left.

Miss Hodges turned back to the class. "What did we learn here?"

Hannah raised her hand. "You can't always trust what you see. Or hear."

"Exactly! Even eyewitnesses aren't always reliable. And with many crimes, there *are* no witnesses," Miss Hodges explained. "That's why we need to collect hard evidence: fingerprints, hairs, fibers, footprints, tire marks . . ."

"Bl-o-o-d-sta-i-i-i-ns?" Ricky asked, drawing the words out to make it sound as gross as possible. One of his buddies snorted.

Miss Hodges considered that. "Yes, sometimes. Or saliva. Human tissue. Stomach contents. . . ."

The class listened, riveted to what Miss Hodges was saying.

Ricky made a loud retching noise, trying to draw attention back to him.

Miss Hodges gave Ricky a quick look and then went on, "In this class you'll learn about how to carefully and systematically gather evidence, scientifically analyze it—sometimes using microscopes and chemicals—and present the results to help solve crimes."

Corey raised his hand, and Miss Hodges called on him. "Before the, uh, incident," he said, "did you say something about having a cousin who works in a Vegas crime lab?"

Miss Hodges nodded. "Yes, I did. Good memory for details. You would make a fine investigator." Corey sat up straight, beaming with pride.

"What did you want to know about my cousin? Or his lab?" Miss Hodges asked.

Corey looked stumped. "Um . . . I forget."

"Class trip to Vegas!" Ricky yelled out. "Vegas rocks!" He liked to let the other kids know he'd traveled beyond the limits of the small Nevada town in which they lived.

"We might be able to go visit, but please raise your hand next time you have something to say," Miss Hodges said, leveling her gaze on Ricky for a moment before continuing. "It's also possible I might persuade him to come here and address the class about his work sometime."

The students murmured excitedly. Las Vegas! Miss Hodges cocked her head and raised an eyebrow. "But don't get the wrong idea," she said. "This class isn't going to be all field trips and guest speakers. We're going to learn the science of crime investigation. And there will be tests."

A couple of students groaned. Ricky rolled his eyes. "Now," said Miss Hodges, turning back to the board, "let's begin with a brief history of forensic investigation. . . ."

After class Hannah, Ben, and Corey walked down the hall, buzzing with excitement about their new teacher and the field of forensics.

"Miss Hodges seems really cool," Hannah said.

"Yeah," Ben agreed. "I'm looking forward to this."

"You mean lunch?" Corey asked.

Ben laughed. "Well, that, too. But I meant the class. I think it's going to be really interesting."

"It's going to be really interesting," Ricky mocked, coming up behind them. "That's just what you would say, dork."

Ben looked annoyed, but held his temper. "Don't you think forensic science is going to be better than earth science, Ricky?"

"No, I don't," Ricky said with a snarl, looking disgusted.

"Why not?" Hannah asked.

Ricky looked around, as though he were checking to see if any teachers were listening. "Because I was gonna cruise through earth science!"

"Cruise?" Corey asked. "But the only thing you know about rocks is how to throw them."

Ricky ignored Corey's comment. "Longfellow used the same tests for thirty years," he said. "I've got copies of everything!"

"Isn't that cheating?" Hannah asked. "And where'd you get them, anyway?"

Ricky sniffed. "I've got my sources." Then he frowned. "But now those copies are totally worthless."

"Too bad," Hannah said. "I guess you'll just have to study."

"Or do something about it," Ricky muttered. He ran ahead to the cafeteria.

"Come on," Corey said. "Let's hurry before all the food's gone. It's burger day, and I'm starving."

They hustled down the hall toward the smell of burgers and fries.

Chapter 2

The cafeteria was already noisy and crowded, but after Hannah, Ben, and Corey got their lunches, they managed to find three seats together near the food line.

Corey bit into his burger, chewed, and swallowed. "All the evidence points to a delicious lunch," he said with a sigh.

Hannah looked thoughtful. "You know, this class could really come in handy. Like, for my career."

Ben looked up from his burger. "What do ballerinas need to know about forensic science?"

"They could solve the Case of the Missing Tutu," Corey suggested. "Or the mystery of how they stand on their toes for such a long time."

Hannah shook her head. "I'm not going to be a

ballerina. That's just what my parents think."

"Then what *are* you going to be?" Ben asked.

"Well, I know I like to help people. So I was thinking about being a police officer," she answered.

"You? A cop?" Corey asked with a small laugh. Hannah glared at him. He reconsidered his question. "Actually, I could see it."

"But now I'm starting to think maybe it would be cool to be a crime scene investigator." She drank from her bottle of water.

Ben said, "Well, I haven't decided exactly what I want to be. But a class in forensic science might look good on my application to MIT."

Corey looked confused. "Isn't that a basketball league?"

"MIT stands for Massachusetts Institute of Technology," Ben explained. "It's a really excellent college."

"Oh," Corey said. "Then what am I thinking of?"

"Food, sports, and the National Invitation Tournament," Hannah answered.

Corey smiled at Hannah. "Swish! Nothing but net!"

Now it was Ben's turn to look confused. "Huh?"

"He means I got it right," Hannah said. "NIT stands for National Invitation Tournament, a basketball tournament."

"Oh," Ben said, slightly exasperated at the sporty turn their conversation had taken. "Anyway, a class in forensic science would show that I have broad interests, but it's still a class in science. College admissions officers like that. I think."

"That's assuming you ace the class," Corey pointed out.

"Why wouldn't I ace the class?" Ben demanded.

"Oh, you probably will," Corey admitted. "Me, on the other hand . . ." He sighed.

"Are you worried about passing forensic science already?" Hannah asked. "After just one class?"

"Well . . . yeah. A little," Corey said. "Miss Hodges made it sound pretty tough. Chemicals and microscopes and analysis . . ."

Hannah gave him a reassuring smile. "Don't worry, Ben and I'll help you. You'll do great! She already said you had a good memory for details."

"She did?" Corey thought a second and then brightened. "Oh yeah! She did!" He took another bite of his burger, and talked with his mouth full.

"I hope you're right. I signed up for earth science, because I heard it was easy. Someone called it 'Rocks for Jocks.' Instead I end up in 'Clues for Geniuses.'"

Ben looked puzzled. "That doesn't rhyme."

"I know!" Corey groaned. "See? I'm not even good at making up a nickname for this class! And if I don't keep my grades up, my parents won't let me stay on the basketball team."

"Relax," Ben said. "Who helped you put together your leaf collection for second grade?"

Corey grinned. "You did."

"And who helped you learn the state capitals in fifth grade?" Hannah asked.

"You did," Corey answered. "I still remember the song you made up." He started to sing, "Oh, Juneau that in Alaska there's a guy named Montgomery from Alabama and he's got a Little Rock—"

Ben held up both hands. "Stop!" he begged. "Please don't sing that song! It'll stick in my head for days!"

"The point is," Hannah said, smiling, "we helped you get through those grade-school projects, and we'll help you get through this junior-high class."

Corey looked a little less worried. "Thanks," he said. "And Miss Hodges seems like a pretty cool teacher, so—"

"Hey, look!" Hannah said. "There she is!"

Sure enough, the new forensics teacher was walking into the cafeteria. She looked around, spotted a stack of trays, and picked one up.

"I guess she doesn't plan on just hiding in the teachers' lounge with a sack lunch," Ben observed.

"Good for her," Hannah said.

"Good for her? These burgers?" Corey asked. "Doubtful. Tasty? Yes. Good for you? Not so much." And with that, Corey took another big bite.

Miss Hodges headed toward the food line and set her tray on the metal sliders. She peered at the food and frowned.

The cafeteria chef and supervisor, Mrs. Collins, walked up to the other side of the counter. She had seen Miss Hodges frown at the food, and she wasn't happy. She looked Miss Hodges up and down. "You must be a new teacher," she said.

Miss Hodges looked up and smiled. "That's right. Miss Hodges. Forensic science."

Mrs. Collins looked unimpressed, but introduced

herself anyway. "Mrs. Collins. I'm in charge of the cafeteria. What'll you have?"

"Well, um . . ." Miss Hodges stared at the burgers, hot dogs, and greasy fries.

"What's the matter?" Mrs. Collins asked.

"Are there any options that are a little more . . . healthy?"

Mrs. Collins looked offended. "This is all healthy."

"Do you have any food that isn't made from red meat?" Miss Hodges asked hopefully.

Mrs. Collins pointed to a container of french fries. "No red meat in these."

Ricky walked up and took the fries. "Thanks, Mom. Can I have another burger?" As his mother handed him a burger, he noticed Miss Hodges. "Oh, hello," he said coolly. "This is my mom. She's in charge of the cafeteria."

Ricky figured it wouldn't hurt to let his teacher know his mom worked at the school. He popped a fry in his mouth and chewed it with his mouth open.

"Is she one of your teachers, Ricky?" Mrs. Collins asked.

"Yeah," he said, still chewing. "Science."

Miss Hodges bit her lip, trying to think of what

to say. She feared she had gotten off on the wrong foot with Mrs. Collins.

"Have you decided what you'd like to eat, Miss Hodges?"

Miss Hodges shook her head. "I don't eat red meat. I guess I'll just have to skip lunch today."

"Suit yourself," replied Mrs. Collins.

Miss Hodges turned to go but then turned back around to face Mrs. Collins. "To be honest, I'm concerned the students aren't being offered a better variety of choices. It would be nice to have some healthier options available. . . ."

Mrs. Collins looked insulted. "Look," she said. "I take a lot of pride in the food I serve here at Woodlands Junior High. A lot of care goes into my food. It's the same food I serve my own family."

"That's right," said Ricky defiantly. "Although, you know, she mixes it up. We won't eat hamburgers or hot dogs at home tonight. Right, Mom? What are we having?"

"Pork chops," she answered. She folded her arms across her chest. "The kids all love the food I serve them. Every day has a theme. And burger day is very popular."

"I'm sure it is," Miss Hodges said. "And I'm sure the food is very tasty, but that doesn't make it healthy."

Mrs. Collins glared at her, and so did Ricky. A few students turned to stare. Sensing she wasn't going to get anywhere with Mrs. Collins on this subject right then and there, Miss Hodges decided to drop it. "Nice to meet you," she said. She turned and walked away without taking anything to eat.

"Well!" fumed Mrs. Collins. "Who does she think she is? Her first day on the job, and she tries to tell me how to cook lunch! Which I've been doing perfectly well for sixteen years!"

"Don't worry about it, Mom," Ricky said. "Something tells me Miss Hodges won't last long at this school." He took a big bite out of his burger.

Back at their table, Ben, Hannah, and Corey watched Miss Hodges leave the cafeteria. "She didn't get anything to eat," Corey said, amazed. "What is she, a robot?"

"I heard her ask why there isn't anything healthy," Hannah said. "She's right about that."

"She may be right," Ben said, "but she sure didn't

make friends with Mrs. Collins. In fact, I think she made an enemy."

As if to prove Ben's point, Mrs. Collins was still scowling behind the counter, muttering angrily to herself. Then she stomped into the kitchen, slamming the door as she went.

"What makes you think that?" Corey asked, winking.

Chapter 3

The next day in class Miss Hodges continued to explain the history of forensic science. "More than a century ago," she began, "a French police officer observed that all criminals leave behind traces of themselves—fingerprints, hair, clothing fibers, tool marks, et cetera. They also take traces with them—paint flakes, carpet fibers, dirt, and so forth. This is called the Locard Exchange Principle."

Miss Hodges wrote "Locard Exchange Principle" on the board. A kid named Jacob raised his hand. "Yes, Jacob?" she asked.

"Has your cousin in Las Vegas ever investigated a murder?"

Miss Hodges looked mildly exasperated. "Yes,

but right now we're discussing the Locard Exchange Principle. Do you have a question about that?"

"Um," Jacob said, thinking. "Did your cousin ever use the Locard Exchange Principle when he was investigating a murder?"

Several students laughed. Miss Hodges couldn't help but smile. "Yes," she said. "He certainly has. He uses it every time he investigates a murder."

"How?" Jacob asked eagerly. The other students leaned forward to hear the answer.

Miss Hodges realized she was going to have to shift gears in her lesson plan. "All right," she said. "Let's set aside history, just for the moment, and imagine that there's been a crime committed here."

"Where?" one girl asked nervously.

"Here in this classroom." Miss Hodges strolled over to the front corner of the room. "Let's say that there's been a murder committed right . . . here." She pointed to a spot on the floor.

"She's right," Ricky whispered loudly. "Last year, in that exact spot, I squashed a bug."

Miss Hodges gave Ricky a look. "I need everyone's full attention. Now, who wants to be the body?"

Corey's hand shot up. He figured it'd be easy to just lie still and pretend to be dead, and maybe he'd get some kind of extra credit.

Miss Hodges nodded to Corey. He got up and proudly walked to the front of the room. She had him lie down on the floor. He thought about twisting his leg into a weird position but then realized it'd be really uncomfortable.

"Watch out for dead bugs," Ricky said. A couple of his buddies laughed. "Who knows if they've washed the floor since last year!"

Miss Hodges shot Ricky another stern look that silenced him. "All right. We have a dead body. What's the first thing we do?"

"Call the cops," Corey said.

"We seem to have a talking dead body," Ben observed.

"Calling the police is excellent," Miss Hodges agreed, "but I meant as a crime scene investigator, what's the first thing you do?"

"Look for clues?" Hannah suggested.

Miss Hodges shook her head. "Not yet. Before you examine the crime scene, you have to secure the crime scene. And why is that?"

"Because otherwise it'll get all messed up," Jacob said.

"According to the Locard Exchange Principle," Ben added, "the murderer must have left traces behind. You don't want other people leaving their traces behind too."

"That's what I said!" Jacob protested.

Miss Hodges smiled. "Excellent. You're both right! That's why the police put yellow caution tape around a crime scene and then try to control who has access to the secured area."

She looked around the room. "Hannah? Please come up and guard the crime scene."

Hannah grinned and got out of her seat. She walked to the front of the class and took a firm stance near Corey. She crossed her arms, hoping she looked official.

"And now," Miss Hodges said, "who would like to try their hand at investigating the crime scene?" A forest of hands shot up. She scanned the room and picked Ben. He walked to the front, looking a little nervous.

"Um, what do I do first?" he asked.

"First," Miss Hodges explained, "show your ID to

24

the officer guarding the crime scene."

Ben took out his wallet and showed Hannah his cafeteria card. Hannah nodded. "Everything seems in order," she said, motioning with her hand for Ben to go ahead.

Ben stepped past Hannah and stood over Corey. Miss Hodges said, "The important thing is to keep your eyes open. You're looking for anything unusual, out of the ordinary."

"Like that you can see the corpse breathing!" Ricky said. A few students laughed. Corey tried to keep as still as he possibly could.

"It's also important to document your investigation," Miss Hodges added. "Ideally, you'd be photographing or even videotaping your search."

Hannah pulled out her phone. "I could take pictures with my phone," she volunteered.

"Good!" Miss Hodges said. Hannah started to take pictures of Ben, even though he was just standing there looking at Corey.

"Get closer, Ben," Miss Hodges suggested. Ben knelt down. "Do you see anything unusual on the victim?"

Ben peered at Corey's shirt. "Just some doughnut

crumbs. But in Corey's case, that's not unusual."

Corey wanted to defend himself, to say he didn't eat doughnuts every morning. But he also wanted to be a good corpse, so he just lay there.

"Still," Miss Hodges said, "food counts as trace evidence. That's why you never eat at a crime scene."

As she spoke, she removed a toolbox from her desk drawer. She took out a pair of tweezers and a plastic bag. She also found a pair of rubber gloves and handed everything to Ben. "All right, Ben," she said. "Put these gloves on and collect your evidence."

Holding the tweezers, Ben moved toward the crumbs on Corey's chest. "You should probably pluck his nose hairs while you're at it," Ricky added. Just about every kid in the class laughed.

"Ricky," Miss Hodges said sternly, "I really can't have you constantly disrupting the class. You are welcome to participate, but if you keep causing distractions and misbehaving, I will give you detention. Next time I have to say something, it won't be just a warning, okay?"

Ricky tried to act like this warning didn't bother him at all, but the other kids could tell he was mad about being singled out.

As Ben collected doughnut crumbs from Corey's shirt, Miss Hodges explained the importance of carefully packaging and labeling the evidence. She also had the other students draw sketches of the crime scene, including the location of the body in the room.

In what seemed like no time at all, the bell rang. As the students got up to leave, Miss Hodges said, "This was a good overview. But there are a lot more steps to a thorough investigation. Next time we'll get into the specifics of different kinds of evidence and then discuss forming a theory of how the crime was committed."

The students filed out. Corey was still lying on the floor. "Um, Corey?" Miss Hodges said. "You can get up now."

Corey popped up. "How much extra credit do I get?"

As Hannah and Ben left the science lab, they heard Ricky bragging to his friend that he'd have Miss Hodges "out the door by the end of the month."

"How are you gonna do that?" his friend asked.

"Hey, when your mom works for the school, you can do anything you want!" Ricky said.

Ben stepped up to Ricky. "What have you got against Miss Hodges, anyway?" he asked.

Ricky stared at Ben and then stepped closer to him. "What have you got against minding your own business, dork?"

Ben didn't back down. "I think it is my business. I like forensic science, and I like Miss Hodges."

"Do you like your teeth?" Ricky asked. "'Cause I think you're about to lose a couple of them."

Hannah got between Ricky and Ben. "Real mature, Ricky. Why don't you grow up and stop being such a bully? You don't scare me."

"Oh, like I'm going to fight a girl," Ricky retorted, sneering.

Corey hurried over to the group, still brushing crumbs off his shirt. "What's going on?" He joined Ben and Hannah, facing Ricky.

When Ricky saw Corey, he hesitated. Corey was a jock and was almost as tall as Ricky. He seemed like maybe he could handle himself in a fight.

"Nothing," Ricky spat. "Your dorky friends were just telling me how forensic science is the greatest

class in the world and how much they love Miss Hodges and how they wish they could marry her."

"Very funny," Hannah said. "So we like her class. So what?"

"So nothing," Ricky answered. "Except that you're all huge geeks."

Ben bristled. He'd been called a geek before, and he didn't care for it very much. "We are not geeks," he said slowly and deliberately.

"Just because we're into criminal investigations, we're geeks?" Hannah asked. Ricky nodded, grinning. Hannah looked at Ben, and she could see that Ricky's taunting was really hurting his feelings.

Hannah's grandpa had once told her that the best way to deal with a bully was to take the wind out of his sails. At the time Hannah was confused by what that meant, but she suddenly knew exactly what her grandpa meant when he had told her that.

"Oh yeah?" Hannah said, looking thoughtful. "Well, I'll tell you just how geeky we are. We're not just going to study forensics in class. Ben, Corey, and I are starting our own extracurricular activity called Club CSI!"

Ben and Corey looked at Hannah and then

each other, in surprise. They were starting a club? This was news to them.

Ricky snorted. "A club? Lame." He turned his back on them and started down the hall. "Have fun in your geek club, geeks!"

Once Ricky was out of earshot, Corey turned to Hannah. "A geek club? I mean, a club? We're starting a club?"

Hannah shrugged. "I just wanted to take the wind out of his sails," she said mysteriously.

"Actually," Corey said, "I think a CSI club could be very cool."

"So do I," Ben agreed. "Hannah, you're brilliant."

Hannah smiled, surprised and pleased. "All right! When should we hold our first meeting?"

"What's wrong with today?" Ben asked.

"Nothing at all. This is an excellent day. And you know why?" Corey said.

"Why?" Hannah asked.

"Because it's pizza day," Corey said. "Let's hit the cafeteria. I'm starving."

Chapter 4

Hannah, Corey, and Ben wolfed down their pizzas so they'd have time for the first meeting of Club CSI before lunch period ended. But they weren't sure where to meet. It had to be somewhere private, but they weren't allowed to just wander into any room in the school.

They settled on an empty hallway near the gym. It had display cases full of old trophies, so there weren't any lockers, and no kids were around. The three friends plopped down on the floor near an exit that nobody ever used.

"This is less than ideal," Ben said, trying to get comfortable by leaning against his backpack. It was so jammed with books that it made a terrible pillow.

"It'll do for now," Hannah said.

"So what's the name of our CSI club?" Corey asked.

"How about that name I told Ricky?" Hannah suggested. "Club CSI."

Corey considered it. "It's got 'CSI' in it. It says we're a club. I like it."

"Okay, that's settled then," Ben said. "We're Club CSI. Now, I was thinking—"

"Who are the officers?" Corey asked.

"Officers?"

"Yeah, you can't have a club without officers," Corey said. "I nominate Hannah for president. After all, it was her idea."

Hannah smiled. "Well, thank you. But since there are only three of us, why don't we start without officers and see how it goes?"

"I don't know," Corey said uncertainly. "I was going to nominate myself for vice president. But I guess we could try it your way."

Ben dug into his heavy backpack for a notebook and a pen. He turned to a fresh page and wrote "Club CSI, First Meeting. (No officers.)" Corey read over his shoulder.

"So you've made yourself the secretary? I thought we weren't going to have officers!" he protested.

"I'm not the secretary," Ben said. "I'm just making a few notes. In class Miss Hodges said it was important to document everything you do."

"But this isn't an investigation," Corey said. "It's a meeting. You just love taking notes."

Hannah rolled her eyes and changed the subject. "So, what's the purpose of Club CSI? Besides showing Ricky we're not afraid to be enthusiastic about something that came out of a class."

The three of them thought. What was the purpose of this club?

"Well . . . ," Ben said slowly, "the purpose of most clubs is to get together for some kind of activity."

"And to enjoy some delicious refreshments," added Corey. He pulled a Granny Smith apple out of his backpack and took a nice, crisp bite.

"What kind of activities did you have in mind?" Hannah asked.

"We could study what we learned in class. Maybe present reports to one another," Ben suggested.

Corey made a face. "Something wrong with your apple?" Ben asked.

"No, with your suggestion," Corey answered. "This is supposed to be a club, not a class."

All three sat there, pondering for a moment. Then Hannah spoke up.

"It seems to me," she said, "that a crime scene investigation club should investigate crimes."

Ben looked concerned. "I don't think the police would like us snooping around crime scenes. Practically the first thing Miss Hodges taught us today was that you have to have proper identification to enter a secured crime scene."

"The first thing she taught us was something about exchanging your locker with the principal," Corey said.

"You mean the Locard Exchange Principle," Hannah gently corrected.

"Oh yeah," Corey said, taking another bite of his apple. "It's hard to remember stuff you learned when you were dead."

Hannah shifted on the hard floor. "I didn't really mean we'd go out and investigate crimes all over town. I thought we'd stick to stuff that happens right here in Woodlands."

"You mean like who stole the chips from my lunch that time in third grade?" Corey said. "I'm still mad about that!"

"You should probably let that go," Hannah said.

"But I had to eat my sandwich with no chips! No chips whatsoever! The criminal should be found and punished!"

"Fine!" Hannah said. "I took them!"

Corey was shocked. "Really?!"

"No," Hannah said. "I just think you should forget about one stupid bag of chips."

"I see," Corey said. "So the mystery goes on. . . ."

Ben tried again to get comfortable leaning on his backpack, but it was impossible. He stood up and paced around the hallway. "I suppose we could investigate school crimes. But even to do that we'd probably need some kind of permission or approval or something."

"Something like . . . an advisor!" Hannah cried. "If Club CSI got Miss Hodges to be our official advisor, we not only would be an official school club, we could also ask her questions about how to do our investigations."

"That's a great idea!" Corey said. "But should we vote? I think clubs have a lot of voting."

"You may be thinking of student council," Hannah said.

"So we all agree: We'll ask Miss Hodges to be our faculty advisor," Ben said. "We could ask her after class tomorrow."

"Why don't we ask her right now?" Corey said.

"But it's still lunch period," Ben said. "We don't even know where she is."

"I'll tell you where she isn't," Corey said. "The cafeteria."

Although Corey was right, and Miss Hodges wasn't in the cafeteria, she did happen to be discussing the cafeteria with Principal Inverno in his office. The principal was a friendly, middle-aged man who'd been doing his job long enough to know how important it was to keep all his teachers happy if possible. A lot of the time it wasn't possible. But he kept trying.

"I know I'm new here, Principal Inverno," Miss Hodges said, "but I thought this was important enough that I wanted to talk to you about it right away."

Principal Inverno smiled. "That's fine, Miss Hodges. I'm always open to hearing new ideas and

suggestions. Now, what's the problem with our cafeteria?"

"It's not so much the cafeteria as the food that is being served to the students," Miss Hodges said.

"You mean the food Mrs. Collins is serving?" he asked, surprised. "I've always found her cooking to be quite tasty. And the students seem to like it. Based on our food bills, they eat plenty of it," he added, chuckling.

Miss Hodges smiled and chose her words carefully. "I'm not saying the food doesn't taste good. I'm sure it does, but then again, I haven't eaten any of it."

Principal Inverno looked even more surprised. "I see," he said. "Go on."

"When I looked at the choices being offered to the students at lunch yesterday for burger day, I was . . . dismayed," she said. "There just didn't seem to be any healthy choices. Burgers, hot dogs— no main dishes without red meat in them. No vegetarian options except french fries, and those aren't very nutritious." She paused for a moment and then went on. "And today was pizza day, with options like pepperoni pizza, sausage pizza . . . Do you see where I'm going with this?"

The principal frowned. He knew Mrs. Collins well, and she was a woman with strong opinions. *Very* strong opinions. On the other hand, he had been reading more and more about the importance of serving students healthy meals. He knew Mrs. Collins used top-quality ingredients and prepared her food with great care, but perhaps that wasn't enough.

"Well," he said cautiously, "what would you suggest?"

"I was thinking that perhaps, as an experiment, we could try having one meatless lunch a week."

"But what would Mrs. Collins serve? Salad?" Principal Inverno didn't think salad would go over very well with the students. Or Mrs. Collins, for that matter.

"Well, I have a wonderful recipe for a meatless meat loaf. It's really delicious," Miss Hodges suggested hopefully. "I could pass it on to Mrs. Collins, and she could try it in place of her usual meat loaf. And then we could make the meatless lunch sound like a really special occasion, so the students would get onboard with the new menu."

The principal consulted the cafeteria meal calendar he kept on his bulletin board and nodded. "Next Monday is actually supposed to be meat loaf day," he said excitedly. "We could call it 'So Good You Won't Even Miss the Meat, Meat Loaf Day'!"

"That sounds terrific!" Miss Hodges said. In her enthusiasm, she spoke a little more loudly than she'd intended to.

Out in the hallway, they heard Corey say, "That's her! She's in there!"

Hannah, Ben, and Corey burst into the office. "Excuse us, Principal Inverno, but could we speak to Miss Hodges for a second?" Hannah asked, a little out of breath.

The principal tried to look stern, but he was always happy when students were excited about talking to their teachers. "You really shouldn't interrupt our meeting," he said, "but luckily, we were just finishing up."

"You want to be our faculty advisor?" Corey blurted out.

"We're starting a club, Club CSI," Ben explained.

"We really like forensic science, and we thought it'd be cool to have our own extracurricular club,"

Hannah added. "But we need an advisor."

Miss Hodges looked a little overwhelmed. Then she smiled. "I'd be honored," she said.

"Great!" Ben said. "Thank you!"

"Oh, and just so you know," Corey said, "the club has no officers. Kind of weird, I know. . . ."

Principal Inverno stood up and smiled. "All right. Now that that's settled, I'd like to get you three to give me your opinion on something."

"Okay," Hannah said. "What is it?"

"How does meatless meat loaf sound to you?"

The three friends looked at one another, puzzled.

Chapter 5

The following week the students of Woodlands Junior High were surprised to see a new banner hanging above the entrance to the cafeteria. It announced, WELCOME TO "SO GOOD YOU WON'T EVEN MISS THE MEAT, MEAT LOAF DAY"! It was a long banner.

As Ben, Corey, and Hannah headed in for lunch, they saw Miss Hodges and Principal Inverno by the entrance to the cafeteria, smiling and greeting students.

"Welcome!" the principal said. "Please enjoy So Good You Won't Even Miss the Meat, Meat Loaf Day!"

"Should we give it a shot?" Ben asked Hannah and Corey.

"Sure," Hannah said. "I didn't bring lunch, so I really don't have any choice."

"Luckily, I'm starving," Corey said, rubbing his stomach.

"That's not luck," Hannah said. "That's normal."

They went in and got trays. But before they could grab some food, Principal Inverno came in and asked for everyone's attention.

"Today is special," he announced, "because here at Woodlands Junior High we're starting something new in the cafeteria." He turned to Miss Hodges.

She said, "From now on the cafeteria is going to be offering healthier choices to you at lunchtime. I think you'll find them not only nutritious, but also delicious."

Standing at the front of the food line, Ricky picked up a plate and sniffed it. "What is this?" he asked suspiciously.

"Meat loaf!" the principal exclaimed.

"Without meat in it," Miss Hodges said proudly. "I gave my special recipe to your mother, and she prepared it." She gestured toward Mrs. Collins. "It looks delicious!"

The cafeteria supervisor managed to give a little nod. She did not look happy about being told what to cook, but the principal had insisted. (He'd also used a little flattery, telling Mrs. Collins she could make anything taste scrumptious.)

"It looks perfect," Miss Hodges said, again trying to placate Mrs. Collins.

Meatless meat loaf didn't sound all that appealing to the students, but everyone was hungry, so they lined up and received their plates with slices of meat loaf. Each slice had some brown gravy poured over it.

After Hannah, Ben, and Corey sat down, Corey eyed his portion. "Call me crazy, but I believe meat loaf should be meat shaped into a loaf."

"This was shaped into a loaf," Ben said. "But then it was sliced."

"Right," Corey agreed. "But there's no meat in it. How can it possibly be meat loaf?"

"Well, think about it," Hannah said. "There's no ham in hamburger."

"There *isn't*?" Corey said, pretending to be shocked.

"Just try it," Ben said. "Tell you what. We'll all take the first bite together. On three. One, two . . ."

All three balanced bites of meatless meat loaf on their forks.

"Three!" They simultaneously popped the meat loaf into their mouths. Then they chewed. And swallowed.

"Not bad," Corey admitted. "Not bad at all."

"I like the gravy," Hannah said.

All around the cafeteria, nervous kids were trying the meatless meat loaf, and all around the cafeteria, kids were surprised to find that they liked it. And that it tasted like real meat loaf!

Miss Hodges looked on, feeling triumphant. "See? It's good, isn't it?"

Lots of kids nodded and gave their thumbs-up. Principal Inverno was thrilled.

Behind the counter Mrs. Collins was scowling. And Hannah noticed that Ricky didn't eat any meatless meat loaf at all.

Still, in the eyes of Principal Inverno and Miss Hodges, So Good You Won't Even Miss the Meat, Meat Loaf Day had been a resounding success.

The day after, on the other hand . . .

Chapter 6

The next day, word spread quickly: A bunch of students had gotten sick to their stomachs after the meatless meat loaf lunch. Principal Inverno even had to go to the hospital for treatment!

Everybody blamed the meatless meat loaf. Some of the parents were furious their children had eaten supposedly healthy food in the cafeteria and it had made them sick. What was going on at that school, anyway? What was in that meat loaf? Who was responsible for this disaster? If it was a school employee, he or she should be fired immediately!

By second period everyone in school was talking about the attack of the meatless meat loaf, including Hannah, Ben, and Corey. Between classes, they shared what they'd heard other people saying.

"Katie told me that a bunch of kids think this is all Miss Hodges's fault," Hannah said.

"Why?" Corey asked, surprised.

"Yeah, why would Miss Hodges poison her own meat loaf?" Ben asked. "That doesn't make any sense. She wanted everyone to like the new healthy food."

"They think Miss Hodges is some kind of crazy health-food fanatic," Hannah explained. "That she included some weird ingredient in her recipe that she thought was good for us, but it turned out to make some people sick. Or that she wanted to make us sick to teach us some kind of insane lesson."

"What kind of weird ingredient?" Corey asked, frowning.

"I don't know," Hannah said. "Like some kind of rare mushroom or something, I guess."

Corey looked panicky. "You mean we ate some kind of bizarre mushroom? Maybe it's going to make us sick too! Maybe it just takes longer on some people!" He put his hand on his forehead, trying to feel if he had a fever.

"Calm down!" Hannah said. "That was just an example. And I really doubt Miss Hodges would

put some sickening ingredient into her recipe. I'm pretty sure she said she'd made it before."

Corey stopped at a water fountain and then drank a bunch of water. He was secretly thinking water might help flush the toxins out of his system.

"I don't think it makes any sense that Miss Hodges did this," Ben said firmly. "She strongly believes in eating a good, healthy diet."

"I totally agree," Hannah said. "But she's really worried about the whole thing. Katie also told me that someone overheard Miss Hodges talking on her cell phone, saying she was afraid she might lose her job over this."

"But then we wouldn't have an advisor for Club CSI!" Corey exclaimed, then added, "And, of course, a teacher for forensic science."

"Miss Hodges isn't the only person afraid of losing her job over this," Ben said. "Mrs. Collins is worried too."

"She seems like a much more likely perp," Corey said.

"'Perp?'" Hannah asked, smiling.

"Short for 'perpetrator,'" Corey explained.

"Yeah, I know," Hannah said. "I just didn't know

anyone had perpetrated a crime. It seems like the food poisoning could have been an accident."

"A very convenient accident," Corey said, his voice full of suspicion. "Did you see how mad Mrs. Collins looked about having to make meatless meat loaf? Some people think she sabotaged the meat loaf because she didn't want anyone telling her how to run her kitchen."

"Maybe," Hannah said uncertainly. "I don't know. Mrs. Collins is awfully proud of her cooking. Even if she were following a recipe she didn't like, it seems like she'd try to do it perfectly."

"Everybody makes mistakes," Ben pointed out. "And she'd never made meatless meat loaf before. Maybe she messed it up somehow."

"Or maybe," Corey said quietly, looking around to see who might overhear him, "her son messed it up for her."

"Ricky?" Hannah asked.

Corey nodded conspiratorially. "Think about it. He hates Miss Hodges. . . ."

"I don't know if he actually *hates* her," Ben said.

"Okay, well, strongly dislikes her. Didn't you say he said he'd get rid of her by the end of the month?"

Ben nodded, admitting Corey was right.

"And even though he acts like a real tough guy," Corey added, "he really loves his mom. If he thought Miss Hodges was being mean to his mom, he might try to do something about it. Like putting something in some meat loaf. His mom probably lets him go into the cafeteria's kitchen whenever he wants to."

Ben still wasn't sure Ricky was the culprit. "But wouldn't he see that putting something in the meat loaf could potentially get his mom in trouble?"

Corey shrugged. "Ricky's no genius. Maybe he didn't think it through. He just thought ruining the meat loaf would get Miss Hodges in trouble, and maybe even get her fired."

Hannah looked excited. "I just remembered something! Yesterday I noticed Ricky didn't eat any of the meat loaf!"

"That proves it!" Corey cried. "He is a guilty perp!"

Ben held up his palms even though it made his heavy backpack slip off his shoulders. "Let's not jump to conclusions. Before we accuse anyone of sabotaging the meat loaf, we should carefully examine the evidence."

"That's a great idea!" Hannah said, excited.

"What is?" asked Corey.

"We should investigate this! It could be Club CSI's first case!" She looked to the two guys for their agreement.

But Ben and Corey weren't sure. This whole meat loaf thing seemed like kind of a big deal. The whole school was in an uproar about it. Parents were mad. The principal was in the hospital. (Some kids said he was being operated on to have meat loaf removed from his stomach because it was stuck there, but that was just a rumor.) Miss Hodges's job was on the line. So was Mrs. Collins's. And if Ricky were behind the whole thing, who knew what he might do to anyone who poked around, investigating?

Still, the whole point of Club CSI was to use forensic science to investigate crimes at Woodlands Junior High. And here was an unsolved crime, practically dropped onto their laps.

"Okay," Ben agreed. "It looks as though we've got our first case."

Chapter 7

In forensic science class, students were dying to talk about the attack of the meatless meat loaf. But Miss Hodges firmly put a stop to all discussion of meat loaf and went ahead with the day's lesson. For once she didn't have to deal with Ricky's interruptions. He stayed quiet and kept to himself.

The students learned about preparing to investigate a crime scene. Miss Hodges showed them the essentials of a simple investigative kit: plastic gloves, camera, and evidence bags.

She also taught them how to plan an investigation of a crime scene. "It's important," she stressed, "to assign each investigator a specific role. You need to be clear about who's going to do what."

Then she had the students try different patterns

of searching a crime scene. They divided the scene into zones and carefully searched each zone. They tried to follow a grid pattern. They also tried a spiral search pattern, starting at the outside of the scene and circling toward the center.

Later that day the members of Club CSI met to start their investigation of the sickening meat loaf. "I think the first thing we should do is investigate the crime scene," Hannah suggested.

"That's great," Corey said. "But how are we going to look inside people's stomachs?"

"In this case," Ben said, "the scene of the crime would be the place where the meat loaf was made—if there was a crime."

"Right," Hannah agreed. "So we need to check out the cafeteria's kitchen."

Corey jumped up, ready to go. "Okay, let's go!"

"Wait!" Ben said. "Miss Hodges said that before officers search a crime scene, they should have a plan for their search, like who's going to do what."

"Right," Corey said, sitting back down. "We might also need some equipment. We should put together a kit."

"That's a great idea," Hannah said.

They decided they'd need rubber gloves, tweezers, plastic bags, labels, flashlights, and a camera. They talked about what they could borrow from home and what they might need to buy.

"I just thought of something," Corey said. "Searching the cafeteria might be a complete waste of time."

"Why?" Hannah asked. "That's where the meat loaf was made, so if anyone sabotaged it, that's probably where it happened."

"I know, but remember what Miss Hodges said about protecting the crime scene?" Corey asked. "Mrs. Collins and the janitor probably already cleaned up the kitchen yesterday, before anyone had gotten sick."

Hannah was impressed with Corey's logic. "That's true."

"It's still worth a look," Ben said. "Lots of times criminals try to clean up crime scenes, but they still leave trace evidence behind."

"But maybe we'd better hurry and check it out before anyone else gets in there," Hannah said.

"Fine, but we'll need permission. And we won't have time to put a whole kit together," Ben said.

Hannah stood up and grabbed her backpack. "We'll just have to improvise. Come on, let's go get permission from the assistant principal."

"Club what?" the assistant principal, Mrs. Miller, asked.

"CSI," Ben repeated. "Crime scene investigation."

Mrs. Miller looked alarmed. She tended to worry a lot. She might have been a little too nervous of a person to handle school administration. "No one said there's been a crime committed. If one had been, we'd call in the police. This was just an accident."

"Actually," Hannah said, "lots of people are saying there's been a crime. Everyone in school is talking about it. And they're trying to guess who might have done it. No one can concentrate on their schoolwork," she added for good measure.

"Oh dear." The assistant principal sighed. "I wish Principal Inverno were here to handle this."

"We just want to help," Corey said. "Maybe if we investigate the kitchen, we can eliminate some of the suspects and stop the rumors."

"*Suspects?!*" Mrs. Miller cried. "I really don't like the sound of that."

"Well, until we can solve this, you're going to hear lots of talk like that in this school—suspects, crimes . . . ," Ben pointed out.

"Revenge, murder, vampires," Corey added.

Mrs. Miller raised an eyebrow.

"Well, maybe not vampires," Corey amended. "Or murder. But revenge is always a possibility."

Mrs. Miller thought for a moment. "Are you an official school club?"

"Oh yes," Hannah said eagerly. "With a faculty advisor."

"And Principal Inverno knows about your club?"

The three friends nodded enthusiastically. "He's known about it almost right from the very beginning," Ben confirmed.

"He's a fan," Corey added.

Mrs. Miller made her decision. "All right. You can investigate the kitchen."

"Thank you!" Hannah said, jumping up and heading out of the assistant principal's office. Ben and Corey followed her.

"But be careful!" Mrs. Miller called after them. "Don't break anything! Or turn on the stove! Or touch the knives! Or make a mess! Or slip and fall!"

The three Club CSI members carefully entered the cafeteria's kitchen. "Remember," Ben said, "try not to touch anything until we all decide it's a good idea. Like if we're gathering a piece of trace evidence."

"Can I gather an apple?" Corey asked. "I'm starving."

"No!" Hannah said. "Remember what Miss Hodges said? No eating at the crime scene."

Corey sighed. "Just my luck. I finally get into the school kitchen, and I can't eat anything. Okay, what are we looking for?"

That was a good question. What *were* they looking for? As they glanced around the room, it looked like a normal cafeteria's kitchen. There was a large refrigerator, a stove, a microwave, a dishwasher, and racks of pots and pans.

"Just keep your eyes open," Ben said a little uncertainly. "Be on the lookout for anything unusual."

"Like a big bottle of poison with a skull and crossbones on the label?" Corey suggested.

"That'd be good," Hannah said. She started to take pictures of the kitchen with her cell phone's

camera. Corey started to walk around the kitchen in a spiral pattern.

Ben noticed there were cutting boards hanging from pegs on the wall. There were three different colors of plastic cutting boards hanging together—red, yellow, and blue. Hannah took a picture of them.

"Check this out!" Corey said. "It looks like Miss Hodges's recipe!" Ben and Hannah examined the piece of paper pinned to a bulletin board. It listed all the ingredients for the meatless meat loaf. Hannah took a picture, which was a lot quicker than copying the recipe by hand.

Near the recipe was a shopping receipt for groceries. Hannah took a picture of it, too.

Overall, the kitchen seemed very well organized and extremely clean. They did find one hair on the counter, which Ben put in a plastic bag with a label that read: HAIR FROM THE CAFETERIA'S KITCHEN.

"Let's look inside the refrigerator," Hannah suggested.

"Should we open it without using our hands?" Corey asked.

"Why?" Ben asked.

"Fingerprints," Corey said.

"We don't have the equipment to lift fingerprints. And Miss Hodges hasn't shown us how to do that yet," Ben said.

"Haven't you already read ahead to the fingerprint chapter in our forensics book?" Corey asked.

Ben looked sheepish. "Well, yes," he admitted. "But we'd need some powders and other special equipment."

"Should I go ask Miss Hodges to help?" Corey asked.

Hannah shook her head. "I don't think we can go to Miss Hodges for help with this investigation."

Corey looked puzzled. "Why not?"

Hannah shrugged. "She's a suspect. At least in some people's eyes. So until the evidence has cleared her, we can't really let her in on our investigation."

Corey looked disappointed. "Shoot. Taking fingerprints would be cool."

"Maybe on our next case," Ben said, smiling.

Hannah opened the refrigerator door and the three of them peered in.

Milk, eggs, ketchup, mustard, barbecue sauce—pretty normal stuff. But on a lower shelf they spotted . . .

"Meat loaf!" the three of them said at the same time. There was one container with a small amount of leftover meat loaf in it. Ben carefully took a sample of the meat loaf and placed it in a plastic bag.

"Whatever you do, don't eat that meat loaf," Corey warned.

"I won't," Ben assured him.

"And I mean even if you're really, really hungry," Corey added. "Like me."

They checked the rest of the kitchen thoroughly. They peered into cabinets. They opened drawers. They even tried checking the trash, but it had been emptied.

Corey thought about scanning the floor for footprints, but it was really clean. "I think they mop it every night," Ben said. "I don't see any crumbs or anything."

Corey agreed. "If there are any mice in here, they must be starving."

Hannah looked in the pantry closet. "I've got an idea! Let's check the recipe and the grocery store receipt to see which ingredients Mrs. Collins had to buy to make the meatless meat loaf."

"Okay," Corey said. "Then what?"

"Then we can take samples of those ingredients

with us," Hannah explained. "If there's more here in the pantry, I mean."

"Great idea," Ben said, turning toward the recipe and the receipt. He called out the ingredients as Hannah and Corey looked for them in the pantry.

"WHAT ARE YOU DOING IN MY KITCHEN?"

Ben, Hannah, and Corey whipped around. Mrs. Collins was standing in the doorway. She looked furious.

"Hello, Mrs. Collins," Ben said, trying to act casual. "Mrs. Miller gave us permission to—"

"*I* didn't give you permission! And this is *my* kitchen!" she snapped. "Students aren't allowed in here. Now get out."

"We're just trying to help," Hannah protested. "We're investigating why people got sick from the—"

"I said get out!" Mrs. Collins shouted, pointing to the door.

The three friends hurried out, taking their samples with them. Mrs. Collins glared at them as they went.

Chapter 8

Ben stuck the meat loaf sample in the science lab's small refrigerator. He didn't want it to spoil. But he hid it far toward the back, since he also didn't want anyone tampering with it. Not even Miss Hodges.

He put the other pieces of evidence in a pocket of his backpack and then zipped it shut. He wished he had some kind of safe to lock them in, but at least he'd have the plastic bags with him at all times.

"Did you see how mad Mrs. Collins was?" Corey asked.

"Yeah, I noticed," Hannah said. "I think it was the way she screamed at us."

"That, my friends," Corey said dramatically, "is the behavior of a guilty person."

"Except she acts like that all the time," Ben said. "Almost makes you feel sorry for Ricky."

"We've got to stick to the evidence," Hannah reminded Corey.

"Speaking of which, what are we going to do next with all the stuff we collected?" he asked.

"Well," Ben answered, "we've got to analyze it as best as we can. I've got a pretty good microscope at home—"

"That's a shock," Corey said, smiling.

"But we're going to need more information, too," Ben continued. "Why didn't everyone who ate the meat loaf get sick?"

"Maybe some of us have a special meat loaf immunity," Corey suggested.

"Maybe," Hannah said doubtfully. "But it'd be good to get a list of everyone who got sick. We could also use some more information on food poisoning."

Corey raised one index finger. "To the Internet!"

Over the next two days, during lunch and after school, the three investigators gathered as much information as they could. They planned to get together and compare their findings. A few of the kids who had gotten sick returned to school, but most stayed home. Principal Inverno, who was out of the hospital but still sick, was still out.

In forensic science class Miss Hodges taught the students about analyzing hairs. She held up a plain yellow pencil. "A strand of hair is similar to a pencil," she announced.

"No wonder mine's so hard to comb," Corey whispered to Hannah, who ignored him. Ben was taking lots of notes.

"The pencil's lead is like the hair's medulla," Miss Hodges said, writing the word on the board. "The wood is like the hair's cortex, and the yellow paint is like the hair's cuticle."

She went on to explain how the cuticle has scales, almost like a fish. Checking the hair's scales helps an investigator decide whether or not a hair is human.

Miss Hodges had the students pluck their own hairs and examine them under the lab's microscopes, paying attention to their color, thickness, curliness, and other characteristics.

"I never realized hair was so complex," Corey said.

In the afternoon the three friends managed to meet up by the trophy cases. Ben shared the list he'd put together of all the people who gotten sick from the meatless meat loaf.

Hannah looked at the list of names for a pattern. "Principal Inverno and ten students. All boys."

Corey looked over her shoulder. "That's weird."

"What's weird?" Ben asked.

"Almost every single one of those dudes is on the swim team," he said. Then he confirmed, "Yeah, all but one of them."

"That's interesting," Ben said. "Maybe we should talk to the swim team."

"That's going to be tough," Corey said. "Most of them are still home sick."

At the indoor pool they found the coach of the swim team teaching a gym class. After explaining why they were there, the coach guessed he could take a second to answer their questions. "Keep swimming laps!" he yelled to the class, his voice echoing in the big tiled room.

After Ben asked, the coach confirmed that the whole swim team had gotten sick. "We had a big meet against Washington Junior High on Monday," he said, shaking his head. "Had to forfeit."

This gave Corey an idea. "Isn't there a big rivalry between our swim team and Washington's?"

"Yep," said the coach. "Has been for years. So that was pretty much our biggest meet of the year. Killed me to forfeit."

"Then isn't it possible," Corey went on, "that someone from Washington did something to make our team sick?"

"You mean it might not have been the meat loaf at all?" Hannah asked.

"Maybe," Corey said. "We've got to keep our minds open to all theories at this stage."

The coach considered this. "I guess it's possible. It does seem like a weird coincidence that the whole team got sick on the day of our biggest meet."

"Could someone have put some kind of bacteria into the pool?" Ben suggested.

The coach looked alarmed for a second. He grabbed his whistle and then started to raise it to his lips to blow, so that he could get everyone out of the pool. But then he lowered it, looking relieved.

"No, that couldn't be it," he said firmly. "Smell that chlorine?"

All three of the investigators nodded. It was easy to smell the strong scent in the air. It hit you the moment you walked through the door.

"Chlorine kills bacteria," the coach explained. "That's what it's for. And I just rechlorinated the pool before the team's last practice. We had a last-minute practice right before lunch."

"Do you mind if we take a sample of the pool water?" Hannah asked.

"Not at all," the coach said. "Go right ahead. But I really don't think you'll find anything. Swimmers are always telling me I overchlorinate this pool. They claim it takes the color out of their swimsuits."

The next day Ben confirmed what the coach had told them. "I couldn't find any bacteria in that pool water at all," he said. "But it had lots of chlorine in it!"

"I guess it kind of makes sense," Hannah said.

"Not everyone who got sick was on the swim team."

"That's right," Corey agreed. "There's Principal Inverno, and that one other kid. What was his name?"

Ben consulted his list of the people who got sick the day after the meatless meat loaf was served. "Dirk Brown."

"Maybe we should go talk to Dirk Brown," Hannah suggested. "He's still out sick."

"Good idea," Corey said. "We could bring him a get-well card."

Dirk Brown sat up on the couch in his family's living room, looking at the card Hannah had just handed him. "Thanks," he said, a little confused. "It's really nice of you guys to come by and give me a get-well card. I'm feeling a lot better. I should be back at school on Monday."

"That's great," Hannah said. "Do you mind if we ask you a couple of questions?"

"About what?"

"Well, we're investigating how you and the others got sick at school," Ben explained.

"Oh," Dirk said, still looking a little puzzled. "Sure. Ask away."

Ben took out his notebook and a pen, ready to write down Dirk's answers. Dirk looked a little nervous about being interrogated.

"Great," Corey said. "First of all, did you swim in the pool at school this week?"

Dirk shook his head. "Nope. I haven't been in that pool since last semester for gym. I don't really like swimming in it. Too much chlorine. Makes my eyes red for the rest of the day."

Ben looked up from his notepad. "Did you eat the meatless meat loaf?"

Dirk nodded unhappily. "Yeah. I did. I'm pretty sure that's what made me sick."

Hannah leaned forward in her chair. "But the part we don't get is, why didn't everyone who ate the meat loaf get sick?"

Dirk shrugged. "I don't know. Who else got sick?"

"The swim team and principal," Corey answered.

"That's who I ate the meat loaf with," Dirk said.

The three investigators looked startled. "What do you mean?" Corey asked.

Dirk leaned back on the couch. His stomach still

didn't feel absolutely great. "I missed the regular lunch period that day because I had a doctor's appointment. I had to eat lunch late. When I went into the cafeteria, the only other people there were the guys on the swim team. They were eating late too, because they'd had an extra practice for some big swim meet."

Ben frantically wrote notes. This new information seemed important. "Oh," Dirk added, "and the principal was there too. He'd already eaten lunch earlier, but he said he just had to have some more of that delicious meat loaf. He really seemed to like it. Took a big piece with lots of gravy."

"Did you like it?" Corey asked.

Dirk shrugged. "It was okay, I guess. But now I don't think I'd ever eat it again."

"Was there anyone else in the cafeteria?" Hannah asked.

"Just the cafeteria lady," Dirk answered.

"Mrs. Collins," Ben said.

"Right. Oh, and I saw her son, too. The big mean kid. What's his name?"

"Ricky," Corey said.

"Yeah, Ricky. He was there too."

The three investigators exchanged looks. They nodded to one another and then got up to leave.

"Thanks, Dirk," Hannah said. "You've been a lot of help."

"I have?" Dirk asked, surprised. "Great. Thanks again for the card. Now if you'll excuse me, I have to go to the bathroom. Again."

Dirk quickly left the room. Ben, Hannah, and Corey showed themselves out.

As they headed down the sidewalk, the three friends started talking rapidly about what they'd learned from Dirk.

"So the people who got sick all ate the meat loaf later, after everyone else did," Ben said.

"Right," Corey said. "But what does that tell us? Does it mean Ricky did it?"

"Why would it mean Ricky did it?" Hannah asked.

"I don't know," Corey admitted. "But Dirk said he saw him there. Maybe he put something in the meat loaf after everyone else had already eaten it."

"I think we need to start analyzing the evidence," Hannah said.

"I know where we can find a microscope," Corey replied.

en's room was full of books and science equipment. Besides his microscope, he had dissection kits, a rock collection, and a chemistry set. In fact, his room smelled a little like the science lab at school. On the wall was a poster of Albert Einstein.

"I wish I had an electron microscope," Ben muttered as he peered through the eyepiece of his microscope. He'd put a tiny bit of the meat loaf on a slide. "With an electron microscope, you can even see viruses. But at least with this microscope, you're supposed to be able to see bacteria."

"Why don't you just run down to the microscope store and pick up an electron microscope?" Corey asked, looking through a magnifying glass.

"Because even the cheapest ones cost, like, sixty thousand dollars."

"Oh. That's a whole lot of lawns you'd have to mow," Corey said. After a moment he asked, "See anything?"

"I'm not sure," Ben admitted. "I've got this on the highest magnification, but I'm not positive I'm seeing anything that could be bacteria."

Hannah was using Ben's computer to look up food poisoning on the Internet. "There are a bunch of different bacteria that cause food poisoning," she said. "I'm not really sure how to say all these, but there's *Staphylococcus*, *E. coli*, *Listeria*, *Salmonella*, *Campylobacter* . . ."

"After this investigation, I'm going to be afraid to eat," Corey said. "Well, maybe." He pulled a granola bar out of his backpack and then crunched off a bite.

"From what I'm reading, *Salmonella* seems like the most likely culprit in this case," Hannah said. "And it seems to like foods that are high in protein."

"Was there salmon in the meat loaf?" Corey asked.

"No, it was meatless, remember?" Hannah said. "Besides, *Salmonella* doesn't have anything to do with salmon. It was named for some veterinarian named Daniel Salmon."

"He discovered the bacteria?" Ben asked, curious. He wouldn't mind having a discovery named after himself someday. "Benjaminella? Benjamineria?" he wondered aloud, until Hannah brought him back to reality.

"Let's see," Hannah said, typing and then clicking something using the mouse. "Um, no. His coworker discovered it."

"So the other guy makes the big discovery, but Salmon gets all the glory?" Corey said, outraged. "I guess Salmon deserves to be a fish who turned into a germ. What's the other guy's name?"

Hannah scanned the screen of the laptop. "His name was . . . Theobald Smith."

"So the bacteria really should be called *Smithella*," Corey concluded.

"And you could call the sickness Theobalding," Hannah added, giggling.

"Or going Theobald," Corey suggested.

Hannah looked slightly annoyed. "That's the exact same joke."

"May I see your phone a minute?" Ben asked her.

"Sure," she said, handing it to him. "But don't look at the saved text messages. Those are private."

Ben scrolled through the pictures on Hannah's

phone until he found the photo of the recipe. "I'd say the meat loaf ingredients with the most protein are eggs and tofu."

"From what I'm reading, either one could be contaminated with *Salmonella*," Hannah said. "It also says there are testing strips you can use to see if food is contaminated with bacteria."

"How do they work?" Ben asked.

Hannah clicked to another screen and then read. "You blend the food with distilled water and a reagent, and then dip in the test strip. The reagent breaks the bacterial wall, releasing enzymes. The enzymes react with the test strips, so they change color, indicating the presence of bacteria."

"I see," Ben said, nodding.

"Oh, yeah, that makes perfect sense," Corey said, baffled. Since they didn't have any of these magical strips, anyway, and had no idea where to get any, he decided to change the subject to something he understood better. "Hey, what about that hair?" he asked.

"What hair?" Ben said.

"The one we found in the kitchen."

"Oh yeah!"

Ben dug through the pocket of his backpack

and found the plastic bag with the hair in it. "Here we are," he said as he carefully removed the hair from the bag with tweezers. He put the hair on a slide, covered it with another piece of glass to hold it in place, and then clipped the slide into the microscope.

He peered into the eyepiece and turned a dial, bringing the hair into focus. "Miss Hodges said we're supposed to examine the follicle, the medulla, the cortex, and the cuticle of the hair."

"Right," Corey said. "What are you writing?"

"Some notes on the distribution pattern of the medulla, the pigment in the cortex, and the cuticle pattern. I wish I had the equipment to do a neutron activation analysis."

"Boy, you took the words right out of my mouth," Corey said. "English, please?"

Ben looked up from the microscope. "I'm taking notes on this hair's color, texture, shininess, and curliness. Then we can see if it matches any of the suspects' hair. That won't positively identify the culprit—you'd need DNA testing for that—but it'd be another useful piece of information."

"I guess that makes sense," Corey said. "But

wouldn't we need hairs from the suspects to see if they match this one?"

Ben nodded. "We sure would."

"But how are we going to get hairs from the suspects?" Corey asked. "I don't think we can just walk up to them and say, 'Excuse me, could I please borrow one of these?' and then yank out a hair."

"I don't know," Ben said. "Maybe that could be your department."

"Collecting hair? How is that a department?" Corey asked. "I think I'd rather be in charge of refreshments. Because so far the snacks at this club's meetings have been pretty pathetic." He popped the last bite of his granola bar into his mouth.

Hannah chimed in. "There are lots of other sources for a suspect's hair. You don't have to pluck it from his or her head. You can collect hairs from a hat. Or a coat. A brush. A comb . . ."

"A bathtub drain," Corey suggested.

"Yes!" Hannah agreed. "That could be an excellent source!"

"If by 'excellent' you mean 'gross,'" Corey said.

"Since when did you get so squeamish?" Ben

asked. "I remember in kindergarten, you ate a worm."

"Yes, but I got paid a nickel to do that," Corey said. "We're doing all this work for free."

"Maybe Miss Hodges will give us extra credit," Hannah suggested.

"Especially if our investigation keeps her out of prison," Corey said.

"You don't really think Miss Hodges did this, do you?" Hannah asked.

"Hey, I'm just keeping an open mind," Corey said. "So far the evidence hasn't eliminated anyone."

That was true. What had they really learned from their investigation up until now? Ben decided to summarize what they had so far. He wrote these points on the dry-erase board hanging on his wall:

- Miss Hodges gave Mrs. Collins the recipe for meatless meat loaf.
- Mrs. Collins fixed meatless meat loaf for the first time.
- Principal Inverno, the swim team, and Dirk Brown got sick.
- They did not get sick from bacteria in the school pool.

- They ate the meat loaf later, after everyone else had eaten.
- The food poisoning might have been caused by *Salmonella*.
- Two ingredients that might have carried the *Salmonella* are the eggs and the tofu.
- There was a hair in the kitchen, but we don't know whose it is.

Hannah and Corey watched as Ben wrote, nodding in agreement as he added each point. It was a good summary of their investigation so far, but it raised a lot of questions. Whose hair had they found? If the meat loaf had *Salmonella* on it, where did it come from? Did someone put it there?

Ben said, "I really think we need to talk to someone who was there when the meat loaf was prepared."

"But the only person we're sure was there is Mrs. Collins," Hannah said, frowning.

"That's right," Ben said, nodding. "Tomorrow's Saturday, but this really can't wait. How about if we pay her a visit at home tomorrow?"

"Oh boy," Corey said. "This should be fun."

Chapter 10

The following day Corey, Hannah, and Ben nervously approached Mrs. Collins's house. It didn't look at all scary. The yard was neat, the bushes were trimmed, and the windows were sparkling clean. It was the person inside the house that made them nervous.

Ben stepped onto the front porch and then rang the doorbell. After a moment Mrs. Collins opened the door. "Yes?" she asked gruffly.

Hannah smiled her friendliest smile. "How are you, Mrs. Collins? We were just wondering if—"

"You three! You're the kids who were snooping around my kitchen at school! What do you want? Why are you bothering me on the weekend?" she demanded.

Hannah gulped. "We, uh, we wanted to, um, ask—"

"We wanted to help you," Corey interrupted.

Mrs. Collins looked confused. "Help me? I don't need any help." She started to close the door.

"So you're not worried about getting fired?" Corey asked.

Mrs. Collins paused. "They wouldn't dare fire me. I haven't done anything wrong."

Ben saw where Corey was going with his question, and chimed in. "But unless the truth comes out, they might fire you by mistake. We just want to figure out exactly what happened so the wrong person doesn't get blamed."

"You know how people are," Corey added. "Always jumping to conclusions. 'Oh, she made the meat loaf, so she must be the one who made everyone sick! We should definitely fire her!'"

"Please?" Hannah added.

Mrs. Collins stood in the doorway for a moment, thinking. Then she held the door open. "Come on in. I'll give you three minutes."

Inside, Mrs. Collins led the club into her living room. It was neat and spotlessly clean. The three

investigators sat on the couch, and Mrs. Collins sat in a soft upholstered chair.

"So," she said, "ask your questions."

The three friends looked at one another nervously, and then Hannah dove in. "What can you tell us about making the meatless meat loaf?"

Mrs. Collins snorted. "There's nothing to tell. That snooty Miss Hodges gave me her recipe. I went out and bought the ingredients I didn't already have. Then I made the meat loaf, and then I served it at lunch."

That seemed straightforward. Nothing new there. But it seemed as though there had to be more to it than that.

"Were there any unusual ingredients in the recipe?" Corey asked. "Like rare mushrooms?"

Mrs. Collins shook her head. "No. The only unusual ingredient was tofu."

Ben asked, "Do you cook meat in the cafeteria's kitchen, Mrs. Collins?"

She looked annoyed. "You know I do. You've eaten it plenty of times."

"Could any of the knives or other utensils that touched the raw meat have touched any of the meat loaf ingredients?" Hannah asked.

"You're talking about cross-contamination," Mrs. Collins said.

"That's right," Hannah said, surprised. She'd learned about cross-contamination while she was researching food poisoning, but it wasn't the kind of term she'd ever heard Mrs. Collins use.

"Look," Mrs. Collins said. "You don't get to run a school cafeteria for sixteen years without knowing about cross-contamination. I'm extremely careful about that. I even have color-coded cutting boards, so everything's kept completely separate."

The kids nodded, remembering the brightly colored cutting boards hanging in the kitchen.

"And I'm certainly aware that you have to be very careful with raw animal products. They can carry all kinds of bacteria," she said.

"Like *Salmonella*?" Hannah asked.

Mrs. Collins nodded. "I thoroughly cleaned every utensil and surface in that kitchen before, during, and after the preparation of that ridiculous meat loaf. I'm confident that neither batch was contaminated."

Hannah looked puzzled. "Neither batch? You made two batches?"

"That's right," Mrs. Collins said firmly. "The swim

coach asked if his swimmers could come eat a later lunch, so I quickly made a second batch for them."

"So it was only the second batch that made people sick!" Corey said, excited. At the mention of her food making people sick, Mrs. Collins scowled. "Allegedly," Corey added hastily.

"Is that everything?" Mrs. Collins asked. "I've got things to do."

"Was the second batch of meat loaf different from the first batch, Mrs. Collins?" Ben asked.

She shook her head. "Same recipe, same meatless stuff. Just a different batch. I prepared it exactly the same way I prepared the first batch."

Club CSI sat on the couch, stumped. If she prepared both batches the same way, why did the second batch make people sick?

"What are they doing here?" Ricky had entered the living room and was shocked to see his classmates in his house. He glared at them.

Hannah tried to strike a friendly note. "Hi, Ricky. We were just talking to your mom."

"About what?"

"The meat loaf."

Ricky looked mad. "Are they bothering you, Mom?"

Mrs. Collins stood up. "It's all right, Ricky. They were just going."

"They'd better," Ricky said menacingly. "Go on."

The three friends stood up. "We're just trying to help," Ben said.

"You think you're so smart." Ricky sneered. "Well, you don't know everything, okay?"

"Was there something you wanted to tell us?" Corey asked.

That was going too far. Ricky looked furious. He stomped over to the front door, holding it open. "Out," he ordered, his voice low and angry.

"Okay, okay, we're going," Corey said as they headed toward the door. "See you at school, Ricky."

"Not if I see you first."

"I've never understood what people mean when they say that," Corey said. "Do you mean you're going to kill me? Or knock me unconscious? Or are you going to hide from me?"

Ricky just stared at Corey, who smiled and waved as he left.

Hannah turned and said, "Thanks, Mrs. Collins," as she went.

The door slammed closed behind them.

Chapter 11

As they walked away from the Collins home, the three friends discussed what they'd learned there.

"Well, for one thing, we learned that Ricky's a jerk," Corey said. "Oh, wait. We already knew that."

"I think we can pretty much rule out cross-contamination," Hannah said. "Mrs. Collins seems really well-organized and superneat. It's hard to imagine her getting bacteria from some raw animal product onto the meat loaf through carelessness."

"Yeah," Ben agreed. "Though anyone can mess up. The really important piece of information was that there were two batches of meat loaf."

"Why is that important?" Corey asked. "She said she made both batches exactly the same way."

"Yeah, but at least it explains why only a few people got sick," Ben said. "Only the second batch was contaminated. But what changed between the first batch and the second batch?"

They walked on, thinking. Then Corey spoke up. "Well, we did get one other thing at Mrs. Collins's house."

"A lot of mean looks from Ricky?" Hannah guessed.

"Nope," Corey answered. "This."

He held up his hand, his index finger and his thumb pinched together. When Ben and Hannah looked closer, they could see that he was holding a hair.

"A hair?" Ben said. Corey nodded, proud to have scored another piece of evidence. "Whose is it?"

"Mrs. Collins's."

"Did you yank it out of her head?"

"No," Corey said. "It was on the chair she was sitting in. I snagged it as I left. I figured we could compare it to the one we found in the kitchen. If they're the same, well, we just found one of Mrs. Collins's hairs in the kitchen. But if they're different, we'll know someone else was in there."

"Nice work!" Hannah exclaimed, patting Corey on

the back. "Come on! Let's get to Ben's microscope."

She took off running. Ben and Corey sprinted after her. Corey held the hair tightly in his hand the whole way.

Ben put the new hair onto a slide and then clipped it into the microscope. "To tell the truth, I'm not even sure I need the microscope. The two hairs look really different, especially the color."

He peered into the eyepiece. "Yeah," he confirmed. "Definitely different. The hair we found in the kitchen is much darker."

"Like Ricky's hair," Corey said.

"It'd be good to compare it to one of his hairs," Hannah commented.

"Yeah," Corey said. "But who's going to get one of Ricky's hairs?"

Ben and Hannah both looked at him. Corey sighed.

"Okay," he said. "I can see I'm going to have an interesting day at school on Monday."

On Monday, Corey got to school early. He stayed outside, hanging around the main entrance, watching for Ricky Collins to arrive.

It wasn't easy, keeping a constant lookout for just one person. Lots of kids were walking into school, and Corey kept seeing people he knew. He had to avoid getting distracted by his friends. He wanted to concentrate on spotting Ricky the second he arrived.

Finally, when it was almost time for the first bell to ring, Ricky slowly came walking up the sidewalk. He was all by himself, wearing a hooded sweatshirt— and a knitted hat! Pulled way down! Over his hair!

How was Corey supposed to pluck one of Rickey's hairs if he was wearing a hat?

Then Corey remembered Hannah saying a hair sample didn't have to come from a suspect's head. It could come from a brush, a comb, a jacket . . . or a hat. Maybe Corey could get a hair off of Ricky's black wool hat. That'd actually be better than yanking it out of his head.

But how was he supposed to get his hands on Ricky's hat? Should he run up, snatch the hat, and sprint away? How could he search the hat for hairs

88

if he was being chased by a big, angry dude?

Just as Corey had made up his mind to snatch the hat off Ricky's head, Ricky pulled his hood over his hat. Great.

Corey followed Ricky into the school, keeping his distance, following him as he made his way to his locker.

Lucky for Corey, the school was kept nice and warm this time of year. In fact, it was a little too warm. As Corey watched him, Ricky pulled his hood off. But he left his hat on. It was now or never.

Corey took a deep breath and then took off like a sprinter from the track team.

"HEY!" Ricky yelled as Corey snatched the wool cap from his head. "Gimme back my hat, geek!"

Corey ran down the hallway with Ricky close behind. He zigged and zagged as Ricky tried to grab him. He tried waiting until the last possible second and then turned corners into different hallways, but Ricky stayed right with him.

As he ran, Corey turned the hat inside out.

Then he got lucky. As Corey zipped past one of the boys' bathrooms, a kid came out—at the perfect moment for Ricky to slam right into him.

"OOF!"

As Ricky untangled himself from the kid, Corey had just enough time to pull three hairs off Ricky's hat! He turned the hat right-side out and tossed it back to Ricky.

"Sorry!" Corey yelled. "I thought you were someone else! The, uh, guy who stole my hat!" Then he ran off.

Ricky was breathing hard. He stopped, picked up his hat, and gasped, "Not funny, dude! NOT FUNNY!"

Once he was sure Ricky wasn't chasing him anymore, Corey stopped. He pulled a plastic bag out of his pocket, putting the three hairs into the bag. Mission accomplished.

Toward the end of lunch period, Ben led Hannah and Corey into the science lab. "Are you sure this is okay?" Hannah asked.

"I got permission from Miss Hodges to use one of the microscopes," Ben explained. "It's fine."

Ben fished the plastic bag with the original hair from the kitchen out of his backpack. Corey pulled the bag with Ricky's hairs from his pocket.

Hannah and Ben put the hairs on slides, being very careful to keep track of which was which. Then Ben examined them under the microscope.

"Well?" Corey asked. "Do they match?"

"For an exact match I'd have to do a DNA test," Ben said. "But take a look for yourself." He gestured toward the microscope.

Corey looked at the hair from the kitchen through the microscope. Magnified, the hair looked as though it had scales, kind of like a lizard. Then he looked at one of the hairs from Ricky's hat. Same scales, same thickness, same color—same everything!

"It's a match!" Corey said. "Ricky must have done it!"

"Done what, exactly?" Hannah asked.

"Put something in the meat loaf!" Corey said, excited. "This proves he was in the kitchen!"

"Not proves," Ben said slowly, thinking. "Strongly suggests, maybe. But that's all it suggests. All we really know is, Ricky was probably in the kitchen. And because his mom works there, he could have been there for a lot of reasons."

"Okay," Corey said, a little disappointed that the

other two club members weren't excited by this new piece of evidence. After all, he'd practically gotten killed gathering the hairs.

"But what was Ricky doing in the kitchen?" he asked.

"I don't know," Ben replied.

"I guess we'd have to ask Ricky that," Hannah said.

"Ask me what?" Ricky asked, standing in the door to the lab. He pointed at Corey. "I've been looking for you."

The three investigators spun around, startled. Corey piped up. "What were you doing in the cafeteria's kitchen?"

"What?" Ricky asked, seemingly thrown for a loop. "When?"

"Last Monday. The day of the meat loaf attack," Corey said.

Ricky slowly walked toward them, shaking his head. "This is unbelievable. First you come to my house and bother my mom. Then you steal my hat. And now you're grilling me like I'm some kind of criminal."

"Well, aren't you?" Corey asked.

"No!"

"You threatened to knock my teeth out," Ben said.

Ricky snorted. "I was kidding!"

"How is that funny?" Hannah asked.

"Look," Ricky said. "We're not talking about some stupid joke I pulled. We're talking about why you're harassing me and my mom! I'm really getting sick of this!"

Corey was impressed. "Harassing" was probably the biggest word he'd ever heard Ricky say. "We didn't mean to harass you," he said. "We're just trying to find out the truth about what happened."

"People are saying my mom might get fired. You know that?" Ricky demanded. For once Ricky didn't just look mean. He looked upset.

Hannah was touched. As tough as he acted, Ricky really cared about his mom. "If you help us figure out what happened, maybe we'll come up with the information that'll keep your mom from getting fired."

Ricky thought about this. "What do you wanna ask me?"

"What were you doing in the kitchen that day?" she asked.

"When?" he asked.

"Later on, when your mom served the second batch of meatless meat loaf to the swim team, the principal, and Dirk Brown," Ben said.

"I don't know who Dirk Brown is," Ricky said. "But yeah, I was there. So what?"

"So what were you doing there?" Corey asked.

Ricky looked away. "Nothing."

"Nothing? Really?" Hannah asked.

"All right, I was helping my mom clean up! Okay?" he barked. "She works really hard. She's there early every morning and has to work hard all day. And so a lot of days, after lunch, I help her clean up the kitchen. Big deal."

He looked down at the floor, embarrassed. It had taken a lot for Ricky to admit he helped his mom with the cleaning. It didn't exactly fit his image as a tough bully.

Corey was confused. He had been sure Ricky did it. "So," he said slowly, "you didn't put anything in the meat loaf?"

"No!" Ricky insisted. "I didn't do anything to that stupid meat loaf. And if people got sick, well, I'm sure it's not my mom's fault. She didn't do anything wrong.

94

She's really good at her job. She's a good cook!"

He headed for the door and then shifted back into bully mode. "Just leave me and my mom alone. Or else. Got it?"

Chapter 12

At the end of the school day, Club CSI met at their old spot in the hallway by the trophy cases. Since Ricky had already barged in on them in the science lab, it seemed best to meet somewhere else to talk about him. Corey plopped down on the floor and leaned back against the wall.

"I gotta admit, Ricky seemed as though he was telling the truth." He sighed. "It's too bad. I was really looking forward to him getting in trouble."

"He seems pretty sure that his mom didn't do it, either," Hannah said, fiddling with a zipper on her backpack.

"That leaves Miss Hodges," Ben said. The other two shot him a look. "Of the original suspects people talked about, I mean."

"I really don't think Miss Hodges would purposefully make a bunch of people horribly sick," Hannah argued.

Corey considered the situation. "I agree. But she might have the know-how, though. Probably knows the best way to stick bacteria on food, so no one would notice."

"Until they got horribly sick," Ben said. "Well, this is all just speculation. We have to go back to the hard evidence."

Corey tossed a ball in the air and then caught it. He often had a tennis ball or even a basketball in his backpack. Tossing a ball and catching it actually helped him think.

"What hard evidence?" he asked. "We've compared the hairs we found, and that basically led us nowhere."

"Well," Ben said, "there are the different ingredients that went into the meatless meat loaf. One of them could have been mishandled."

Hannah consulted her notes. "We said the two most likely ingredients to carry *Salmonella* were the eggs and the tofu."

"Did Mrs. Collins buy the eggs that day?" Ben asked.

Hannah searched through the pictures on her

phone. She found the photo of the grocery store receipt and then zoomed in on it. "Doesn't look like it. I don't see any eggs listed on the receipt."

"Then she must have already had them. Eggs are a common ingredient people have in their fridges, and I bet she uses them all the time. Did Mrs. Collins serve anything with eggs in it the Friday before?"

"I have no idea," Hannah said.

"Does cake have eggs in it?" Corey asked.

"Usually, yeah," Hannah said.

"Then, yes, Mrs. Collins did serve something with eggs in it the Friday before—yellow cake with white frosting," Corey said confidently.

"You remember that?" Hannah said, amazed.

"I have an excellent memory, remember?" Corey reminded her.

"And nobody got sick from that cake," Ben said. "So we can conclude that the eggs must have been okay."

"It all comes back to the tofu," Corey said dramatically.

"It could be," Hannah said, pondering this possibility.

"I have just one question," Corey said.

"What's that?" Ben asked.

"What exactly is tofu?" Corey asked. "It sounds like something you find between your toes. No wonder people got sick."

"I can't believe you don't know what tofu is," Hannah said.

"I couldn't believe you didn't know what a pick-and-roll was, either," Corey countered. "But you didn't. Until I showed you. Now every time you watch a basketball game, you're like, 'Nice pick-and-roll.'"

Hannah smiled. "Okay, fine. Tofu is fermented bean curd."

"Mmm, nothing says good eatin' like curd," Corey said, rubbing his stomach. "What kind of beans?"

"Soybeans," Ben said. Even though Hannah was explaining tofu to Corey, it was very difficult for Ben not to answer a question when he knew the answer. That was something he was working on— letting other people give the answers to questions. He wasn't doing all that well.

"So you take some delicious soybeans, and then you let them curdle until you have some yummy, yummy tofu," Corey said. "What does it taste like?

I thought the meat loaf just tasted like meat loaf. It didn't taste like beans. . . ."

Ben started to answer but then let Hannah speak. "It doesn't have much flavor of its own," she said. "But it's good at picking up other flavors. And it's full of protein."

"But doesn't *Salmonella* usually come from animals?" Ben asked. "Tofu is completely vegetarian."

"Yes," Hannah confirmed. "But tofu can have *Salmonella*. Sometimes it's stored in water, and the water can easily be contaminated."

Corey made a face. "So tofu isn't just curdled soybeans. It's wet curdled soybeans? Why hasn't it been banned?"

"You should probably try it again before you make up your mind about tofu," Hannah said. "It's actually pretty good. I've had it in Chinese food. The place at the mall makes a really yummy tofu in brown sauce dish that I bet you'd love."

Ben had gotten out his notepad and was taking notes. "So you were saying that sometimes tofu is packed in water, and the water could be contaminated?"

Hannah nodded. "Right. You can buy tofu

different ways—in a sealed dry package, in a sealed package in water, or even in bulk, floating in water." She recited the details from memory. Corey wasn't the only one with a good memory!

"Somehow, the more you describe it, the worse it sounds," Corey said.

"It also comes in four different textures—silken, soft, firm, and extra firm," Hannah said, this time checking her notes to make sure she was remembering all the details.

"Which texture is the most prone to contamination?" Ben asked. He thought they might really be on to something with this tofu.

"I'm not sure," Hannah said. "But from what I've read, it seems as though you'd probably use firmer tofu in a meatless meat loaf. To make it more, you know, meat loaf-y."

"Are there lots of different kinds of tofu?" Ben asked.

"Oh yeah," Hannah said. "All kinds of flavorings are added to tofu, at least in Asia. There's sweet almond tofu, red pickled tofu, and—you'll like this one, Corey—stinky tofu, which is fermented in fish brine. It's supposed to smell terrible."

"Yeeech," Corey said. "Disgusting."

"But Mrs. Collins probably just used regular plain tofu, right?" Ben asked.

"I think that's what Miss Hodges's recipe calls for," Hannah said. "Just plain old regular tofu."

Corey tossed his ball so high, it almost hit the ceiling. "Okay, as much as I'm enjoying this discussion of the wonderful world of tofu," he said, "what are we going to do next?"

Hannah and Ben thought for a minute. That was a good question. They weren't really sure how to proceed at this point. It'd be nice to ask Miss Hodges for her advice, but they'd decided not to include her in this investigation, since some people considered her a suspect.

"I guess I could take another look at the meat loaf sample under the microscope," Ben suggested, even though he didn't have much faith that he would find anything new in the sample. "Or try to run some kind of test on it."

"Like what?" Hannah asked.

"I don't know," Ben admitted.

"Where did the tofu come from?" Corey interrupted.

Now *that* was a good question. Hannah looked

through her photos from the cafeteria's kitchen and found the one of the receipt. "Mrs. Collins bought it that morning," she said. "At Stan's."

They all knew Stan's. It was a small family-run grocery store not too far from Woodlands Junior High. Stan's had been around as long as any of them could remember. It was pretty close to their grade school, too, and they'd gone there sometimes after school to buy candy. In fact, Corey still stopped in there sometimes to grab a snack.

"They have tofu at Stan's?" Corey said. "Now I'm not sure I can go there anymore."

Hannah held up her phone. "According to the receipt, they do."

Ben was encouraged. This seemed like a much better lead to investigate than going back to the meat loaf sample. "We should go there. Maybe they accidentally sold Mrs. Collins some bad tofu. In a grocery store, there are probably plenty of opportunities for cross-contamination, if you aren't careful."

Hannah stood up. "Let's go right now."

Corey shook his head. "Can't. Basketball practice."

"Oh," Hannah said, disappointed. She was eager to follow up on the tofu right away.

"You could go ahead without me," Corey said. But something in Corey's voice, and his face, told Ben and Hannah that he didn't really mean that. They exchanged a quick look.

"No," Ben said. "We work as a team. We can wait to go till tomorrow morning."

"And if we went without you," Hannah said, "we might miss out on you asking a good question."

Corey perked up. "I ask good questions?"

Hannah smiled. "Sure, when you're not asking bad ones," Hannah joked. She saw Corey's face fall a little, and she quickly added, "You're the one who thought to ask where the tofu came from, remember? We need you there!"

"All right!" Corey said, heading off to basketball practice. Then he turned back. "Here's a good question for you."

"Yes?" Ben said.

"How early tomorrow morning?"

Chapter 13

lub CSI got together very early the next morning, since they had to check out Stan's before school. Luckily the little grocery store opened up at six. To compete with the big chain stores, Stan's had to do everything they could to keep their customers happy.

As they walked through the cool morning air, Hannah asked Corey how basketball practice went. "Did you guys work on your pick-and-roll?" she asked, smiling.

"As a matter of fact, we did," Corey answered, yawning so wide that he thought his mouth might split. "But it wasn't my greatest practice ever. Coach yelled at me for not staying focused."

"What were you thinking about?" Ben asked.

"Believe it or not," Corey said, yawning again, "tofu."

Ben and Hannah laughed.

"Somehow I couldn't get it out of my head," Corey said. "Especially the stinky tofu made in fish brine. I actually had a dream about it last night."

"Dream . . . or nightmare?" Ben asked, chuckling.

"You're right, it was a nightmare," Corey said. "A tofu nightmare. I dreamed I was playing basketball. I set a pick and then signaled the guy with the ball that I was open. He threw me the ball, but when I caught it, it was a big, wet, smelly ball of tofu. I looked at the player who passed it to me, and he was a fish. In a basketball uniform."

Hannah and Ben were laughing pretty hard at this, but Corey went on describing his dream.

"The fish looked right at me and said, 'Go ahead. Stuff it in.' I said, 'The basket?' And he said, 'No, your mouth.' I was about to eat the ball of tofu when I woke up with my pillow in my mouth."

This made Hannah and Ben laugh even harder.

"It wasn't funny," Corey insisted. "It was scary."

Hannah and Ben kept laughing.

"Okay, I guess it was a little funny," Corey confessed.

"Not only is the dream funny," Hannah said, catching her breath, "it's also pretty hilarious that you try to eat in your sleep too!"

They reached Stan's. It was the only business around. The rest of the buildings were houses and apartment complexes. Stan's dated back to a time when you could still open a business right in the middle of a residential neighborhood.

There was nobody parked out front. Things seemed quiet at the grocery store.

The doors slid open, and the trio walked in. Stan's had that grocery store smell: a mix of fruit, vegetables, cardboard, and air-conditioning. They looked around for an employee. Stan's never had a lot of people working, but this early in the morning, there was hardly anyone there at all.

Ben spotted a cashier in an apron near one of the checkout lanes. She was rearranging the magazines on a rack.

"Excuse me," Ben said.

The cashier looked over and smiled. "Yes?" she asked, walking toward them.

"Do you think we could speak to the manager?" he asked.

"Sure," she said. "But if it's about applying for jobs, forget it. He's not hiring."

"No, it's not about a job," Hannah assured her.

"It's about tofu," Corey said.

The cashier looked puzzled, but pointed toward a door at the back of the store. "He's in his office."

"Thank you," Ben said politely. "Oh, um, could you tell us where the tofu is?"

"Sure thing," she answered. "Aisle six. On the right."

"Thanks," Hannah said.

"Have fun," the cashier said, giving them a slightly confused smile.

On their way to the manager's office, Ben, Corey, and Hannah stopped to look at the tofu. It was in an open refrigerated case.

"They're keeping it refrigerated," Corey said. "That's good, right?"

Hannah picked up one of the packages of tofu. "Yes, that's good. It's packed in a sealed plastic container, so that's good too."

"Check the sell-by date," Ben suggested.

Hannah turned the small package around in her hands until she found the date. "It's fine," she reported. "Several days from now."

Corey looked at the few tofu containers in the case. "Not a whole lot of it, is there?"

"No," Ben agreed. "Not that much."

"That's not too surprising," Corey said. "I mean, how many people eat this stuff, anyway?"

"You did, for one," Hannah reminded him. "In meat loaf form."

"True," Corey said. "But that was complete ignorance on my part. I really had no idea what I was eating."

He picked up one of the tofu packages. "I thought you said there were lots of different kinds of tofu. These all look the same."

Hannah shrugged. "I guess they carry only one kind."

"Come on," Ben said. "Let's go talk to the manager."

They walked to the back of the store. Hannah gently knocked on the office door. A man's voice said, "Come in."

Hannah opened the door. A tall, dark-haired man was sitting in a chair at a desk covered with papers and an old desktop computer. He turned around in his chair. "How can I help you?"

"Are you Stan?" Corey asked.

"No, I'd have to be pretty old to be Stan," he answered. "He was my grandfather."

He swiveled in his chair and then pointed with his thumb toward an old framed photo hanging on the wall. It was of a group of men and boys standing in front of the grocery store.

"He's Stan. These two men standing next to him are my father and my uncle. And these two boys are me and my brother."

He turned back to face them. "So I'm not Stan. I'm Jack. But I run Stan's."

"Does your brother work here too?" Hannah asked.

"No," Jack said. "He, um, moved away. I'm the only member of the family left here in Grandpa's store. I'm in charge of purchasing, marketing, accounting, and, now and then, mopping the floors."

"That's why we wanted to talk to you," Ben began. "We're Club CSI from Woodlands Junior High School."

Jack looked confused. "CSI?"

"We just wanted to ask you about some tofu you sold recently," Hannah explained.

"Something wrong with it?" Jack asked, frowning.

"That's what we're trying to find out," Ben said. "Our cafeteria supervisor, Mrs. Collins, bought tofu here to make meatless meat loaf."

Jack thought a moment. He then nodded, remembering. "Oh, right. I remember her. Didn't seem real thrilled with the idea of making meatless meat loaf. She came in with a list of ingredients she needed to buy early that morning. I recognized her. She's been shopping here for years. Not for all the school's food, unfortunately. But when she needs something kind of unusual, she'll come in. I think it's because we're close to the school, and she knows we'll help her find things. We'll even deliver. The big grocery stores won't always do that. Or if they do, they charge you for it! They don't care about customer service the way I do. . . ."

"And you helped her find the tofu?" Ben asked, bringing the conversation back on track.

"Right," Jack said. "Bought all we had."

"But you've got some out there now," Corey said.

"New shipment," Jack explained.

"Did you deliver the tofu to the school?" Hannah asked.

"No, she took it with her," he answered. Jack

then asked, starting to turn back to his paperwork, "Is that all you needed to know?"

"One more thing," Ben promised. "We looked at Mrs. Collins's receipt, and it seems as though the amount of tofu she bought wouldn't be enough to make meatless meat loaf for the whole school."

Jack nodded. "Yeah, I don't have room in the case to carry a whole lot of tofu, and there isn't that much demand for it here."

"Or maybe anywhere," Corey added.

Ben looked puzzled. "If you didn't have enough tofu for Mrs. Collins, I wonder where she got the rest of it."

"I happen to know the answer to that," Jack said. "When Mrs. Collins mentioned that she'd need more tofu, I called the new health food store over on Silver Street. They had what she needed, so she said she'd get the rest from there."

"Wow," Hannah said. "That was nice of you, sending someone to a competitor."

Jack shrugged. "Anything for the customer."

"Hey, I've heard of that health food place," Corey said. "My mom was talking about it. She was saying that it was really nice inside, and it was doing great business. I heard her telling my dad that it was probably going to take a lot of business away from Stan's."

Then Corey remembered who he was talking to. "Oops."

A quick scowl flashed across Jack's face. "You know, that place is part of a giant chain. And the chain isn't even owned by Americans. The owners are this huge European corporation. I don't know what people are thinking when they decide to give their money to—"

Jack stopped himself. He took a breath and then smiled. "Well," he said, this time in a voice that sounded a little too cheerful, "a little friendly competition never hurt anyone. And like I said, that's where I sent Mrs. Collins to buy the rest of her tofu."

"Maybe we should go talk to someone at the health food store," Ben said.

"Sounds like a good idea," Jack replied, then added, gesturing toward all the papers covering his desk. "Now, unless there's anything else I can help you with, I'm afraid I've got a lot of work to do. As you can see."

Club CSI thanked Jack and then left him to his work. Once they were outside, Hannah asked,

"Should we go to the health food store right now?"

Ben looked at his watch. "No, we've got to get to school," he said. "Is after school all right?"

"Yep," Corey said. "No practice today. But it won't be easy."

"Why?" Hannah asked as she headed down the sidewalk toward school.

"Right after school is when I'm at my hungriest," Corey explained. "And this place is, you know, a health food store." He made a face.

Hannah laughed. "I think you'll survive."

Chapter 14

In forensic science class later that day, Miss Hodges took the students through a unit on facial characteristics. She explained that sometimes investigators have to determine whether two photographs are of the same person, even if years have passed between the pictures.

"You can grow a beard or get a tattoo," she said. "But unless you get some pretty serious surgery, the bones in your face will stay the same." She explained how the ridges under your eyebrows, cheekbones, chin bones—even the shape of your nostrils—can help an investigator match two pictures of you.

She passed out pictures and had the students carefully examine them to figure out which ones were of the same people—if any. It was tricky, but if you really looked closely at the pictures, and managed to keep them in your mind, it was possible to match up some of them.

One of the hardest pairs to match was of a guy when he was a kid and when he was a grown man. Only Ben caught that one.

After school the three investigators met by Hannah's locker. As they were heading out, they passed Miss Hodges in the hallway. "Hi, Miss Hodges!" Hannah said. "Great class today!"

"Thanks, Hannah," Miss Hodges said, smiling a little. "Let's hope it won't be my last."

Ben looked worried. "What do you mean?"

"Oh, I probably shouldn't say anything," she said. "But I doubt it matters much now. Principal Inverno will be back in school tomorrow."

"That's good," Corey said, puzzled.

"Yes, he's finally well again, so that's great," Miss Hodges agreed. "But he wants to meet with me and Mrs. Collins first thing in the morning. I'm sure it's about the meatless meat loaf. Anyway, I—I shouldn't be talking about this with you. Don't worry. And thanks for telling me you enjoyed class! Have a nice evening."

Before they could say anything else to her, Miss Hodges turned and then walked into the science lab, closing the door.

"Poor Miss Hodges," Hannah said. "She seems really worried that she's going to get fired."

Ben looked determined. "We've got to solve this case before tomorrow morning—before Principal Inverno does anything drastic."

"Then we should get over to that health food store right away," Corey said. "Coach says I need to work on my conditioning, anyway, so . . ."

He took off running. After a second, Ben and Hannah ran after him.

The new health food store—along with a dry cleaner, a sporting goods store, and a place that sold pool supplies—was located in a strip mall on Silver Street. The parking lot was full, and the health food store seemed busy. Lots of people were going in carrying empty cloth bags. Others were coming out carrying cloth bags full of fruit, vegetables, and other organic food.

"Maybe I'll just check out the sports store real quick," Corey said, heading toward it.

Hannah grabbed his arm. "You can go in there

after we talk to the manager at the health food store. Come on."

Inside, the store was bustling with customers. Everything was beautifully displayed and well lit. Ben asked an employee if they could speak with the manager.

"You're in luck," he said. "You can talk with the owners. They're in the back."

As the employee led them through a door and into the back of the store, Corey whispered to Ben, "The *owners*? Are we going to talk to a bunch of guys in business suits?"

But the owners of the health food store turned out to be a friendly middle-aged couple, Bill and Laura. They were casually dressed, and they seemed perfectly happy to answer any questions about their new store.

"It's a nice day, so why don't we talk outside?" Bill suggested. They followed him to a tiny yard behind the store, where employees could sit at a picnic table for lunch or if they wanted to take a break. Everybody sat down, the owners on one side of the table and the investigators on the other side.

"So, what would you like to know?" Laura asked.

"Are you doing a report for a class?"

"Or your school newspaper?" Bill guessed.

Corey thought those might be good cover stories for the future. He mentally filed these ideas away, hoping he'd remember them.

"No," Ben said. "This is for school, but it's not a report. More like a project."

Corey thought that was a good cover story too.

Ben explained how they were taking a forensic science class at Woodlands Junior High School and how the three friends had formed Club CSI.

Then Hannah jumped in, giving a little background on the attack of the meatless meat loaf.

"Oh dear," Laura said, looking anxious. "Did someone buy the ingredients for that meat loaf here at our store?"

"Just one of the ingredients," Ben said. "The tofu."

"I see," Bill murmured, a serious expression on his face.

"What kind of tofu do you sell here?" Hannah asked.

"A couple of different kinds," Laura said. "We have it in small plastic packages that are sealed.

Many of our customers buy it that way because they don't need large amounts. We also sell it in bulk."

"You mean in barrels of water?" Ben asked.

"Yes," Laura said. "Just like in an authentic Asian market."

Ben and Hannah exchanged a look. "You know," Hannah said, hesitating a little, "we've been doing a bunch of research on tofu. And we've read that it's tricky, making sure that tofu stored in open containers of water isn't exposed to any kind of contamination."

"You have to be really careful to make sure no bacteria get into the water," Ben said.

Corey was afraid that Bill and Laura might be offended by Ben's comment. Sometimes he could be a little blunt. He could even sound like he was lecturing you, if you didn't know him well enough.

But the owners remained perfectly friendly. "You've really done your homework," Laura said, impressed. "And you're right. You have to be especially careful with tofu stored in open containers of water."

"And we are," Bill added. "Very careful. It's one of the first things we teach our employees. The tofu has to stay at a low, refrigerated temperature the whole time, and so does the water it's in."

"Come on," Laura said. "We'll show you."

They got up and went back inside. Bill and Laura led them through the small back storage area to the wide doors that suppliers used to deliver food.

"The tofu arrives in a refrigerated truck," Bill explained. "So it's cool when it gets here. We immediately bring it into this cooler." He opened the door to a large walk-in cooler, but not before pointing to a thermometer on the outside of it.

"We constantly monitor the temperature to make sure it stays cool enough in here," he continued as the group walked into the cooler.

"Chilly," Corey said. "Must be nice on a hot day."

Laura laughed. "Yes, on really hot days we all think of chores that need to be done in the cooler."

Bill pointed to a plastic container of water. "This water has been waiting in the cooler, getting down to the right temperature for the tofu. Once we know the cooled water has reached the correct temperature, we put in the tofu. Then we carry the container of water and tofu out to the refrigerated case in the store's bulk food area. Follow me."

They went with Bill and Laura back into the store, following them to the bulk food section. In a refrigerated case, there was a container of tofu in water. The case also had a large thermometer, so that the temperature could be checked.

"So as you can see," Laura said, "the tofu stays nice and cool—and safe—throughout the whole process."

"And some of our customers love being able to buy their tofu in bulk. They can get the exact amount they want," Bill said.

"Great," Corey said, wrinkling his nose.

But the three investigators were stumped. If the health food store was so careful with their tofu, how had bad tofu gotten into the meatless meat loaf and made people sick? Were they wrong about the tofu after all? Had all this questioning been for nothing? It was looking bad for Miss Hodges's job. . . .

Then Corey thought of something. "Do you remember selling a bunch of tofu to Mrs. Collins from Woodlands Junior High recently? Jack from Stan's grocery called to ask about it, and then she came over to buy it."

Laura and Bill both thought, trying to remember.

"I don't think so," Laura said, shaking her head. "And I don't remember ever talking to anyone from Stan's on the phone. The management at Stan's has been less than friendly to us . . . ," she started to say and then stopped herself. "Bill, does that ring a bell for you?"

"No, I don't remember that," Bill said. "But maybe one of our employees took the call and then helped her."

"What day was this?" Laura asked.

"Last Monday," Hannah answered.

"Okay, let's see who was working that day," she said, leading them to a tiny office area.

Bill went to sit at a small desk and used a mouse to click on the screen at a desktop computer. "Last Monday," he muttered. "Let's see. Well, Jim was working that day. He's a new employee. And he's here today."

"May we talk to him?" Ben asked.

"Sure," Laura said. "I think I saw him back in the stocking area."

The five of them walked over to the stocking area, where they found Jim unloading a carton of nuts.

"Hey, Jim," Bill said, giving a little wave.

"Hey," Jim answered, not looking up from his work.

"These young folks would like to ask you a couple of questions," Bill announced.

"Okay," Jim said, straightening up and looking at the kids for the first time. He seemed a little wary. "What about?"

Hannah spoke up. "Last Monday, did you take a call from Jack, the manager at Stan's, about a woman who wanted to buy tofu?"

Jim nodded slowly. "Last Monday? Let's see . . . yes. Yes, I believe I did. I was working in the meat department when Jack called."

"And you helped the woman with the tofu?" Ben said.

"Yeah," Jim said. "They told me how much she needed, so I went straight to the bulk tofu and got it out, so it'd be ready for her."

"So you took it out of the refrigerated case?" Hannah asked.

"Yeah," Jim confirmed.

"And where'd you leave it?"

"Up front," he said.

With each of Jim's answers, Bill and Laura were

looking more and more dismayed.

"How long did it take the woman to get here to buy the tofu?" Corey asked.

"I don't know," Jim said, shrugging. "Maybe half an hour. Maybe more. I think she had some errand to run in-between or something."

"And sorry for asking this," Ben said, "but after you left the meat department to get the tofu, did you wash your hands?"

"I really don't remember," Jim said. "Probably not. I was in a hurry."

"Probably *not*?" Bill said.

"Jim," Laura said, growing more upset by the second. "Don't you remember us telling you how careful you had to be with the tofu?"

Jim shook his head defiantly. "No, I don't remember that. All I ever remember was you telling me to move faster, because time is money." He turned to the kids. "Making money seems to be the only thing they're interested in."

Bill and Laura looked shocked. "That is not true!" Bill insisted. "We have stressed cleanliness, safety, and customer service every day since we opened this store!"

"Okay, fine," Jim said. "Have it your way."

"This is unbelievable!" Laura said. "Jim, we need to talk with you in the office. Right away." She pointed to the office door and then turned back to Ben, Corey, and Hannah. "I assure you, this is not the way we run our business. If our tofu made anyone sick because of this employee's negligence, we are truly sorry. And we will make things right."

"Now if you'll excuse us," Bill said, "we need to have a talk with Jim."

Outside the store, Club CSI wasn't sure who to believe, the owners or Jim. But they knew they felt really proud.

"We did it!" Corey said. "We tracked down the bad tofu! Assuming, of course, that there's such a thing as good tofu. Which I still kind of doubt."

"We've got to tell the principal first thing in the morning," Hannah said excitedly. "This clears Miss Hodges completely."

"Agreed," Ben said quietly. He seemed to be thinking about something.

"What's up with you?" Corey asked. "Aren't you excited?"

"Yeah, of course," Ben said. "I was just trying to remember where I'd seen that guy before."

"Which guy?" Hannah asked.

"Jim," he said.

Chapter 15

Principal Inverno sighed. He usually enjoyed his job, but today was one of those days when he was going to have to criticize someone for making a big mistake. In fact, he was probably going to have to fire someone. He was not looking forward to that.

He had called Miss Hodges and Mrs. Collins into his office first thing that morning. With something you didn't like doing, it was better to get it over with as soon as possible. That way, you didn't have to spend the whole day dreading it.

Mrs. Collins arrived first. Her jaw was clenched tight, and her eyes were narrowed. "Good morning," she managed to say. "Welcome back."

"Thank you," he said.

"You're feeling better?" she asked.

"Much better, thank you," he said. "Please sit down."

Mrs. Collins sat. They waited for Miss Hodges, who arrived a couple of minutes later. She and Mrs. Collins exchanged a look. Mrs. Collins looked mad. Miss Hodges's expression was harder to read. Maybe a little angry. Or maybe apologetic.

Miss Hodges also asked how Principal Inverno was feeling. Once that was out of the way, they had to get down to business.

"Well," the principal began, "I think you both know the reason why I called you in here. I want to—"

The door swung open and Ricky burst into the office wearing his hooded sweatshirt and knitted cap. "You can't fire my mom! She didn't do anything wrong!"

"Ricky," the principal said, trying to be patient, "this is a private meeting. I know you're concerned about your mother, but you were not invited."

"If you wouldn't mind, I'd like for my son to be here," Mrs. Collins said.

"That's fine with me," Miss Hodges interjected.

Surprised, Mrs. Collins gave her a quick, grateful look.

Principal Inverno puffed his cheeks and then blew out air. "Okay," he said. "You can stay. But no outbursts."

Ricky slid into a chair next to his mom.

"What happened last week is a serious matter," the principal said. "Several students became quite ill, and their parents are very upset. They want answers. So I need to find out exactly what went wrong on So Good You Won't Even Miss the Meat, Meat Loaf Day."

"I just followed the recipe," Mrs. Collins said. She tilted her head toward Miss Hodges. "Her recipe."

"That's right!" Ricky said, leaning forward in his seat.

"Ricky," the principal said with a warning tone. Ricky sat back. The principal then addressed Mrs. Collins. "And you're confident that you followed the recipe exactly, with fresh ingredients?"

Mrs. Collins nodded. "I went shopping for them that morning."

The principal turned to Miss Hodges. "I have a lot of confidence in Mrs. Collins. She's been working here for sixteen years, and no student has ever gotten sick from her cooking before. Her kitchen is inspected regularly, and it always passes with flying colors."

"It's obvious she takes her job very seriously," Miss Hodges said sincerely.

"Yes, she does," the principal agreed. "And I think you do too. But you are a science teacher. When you decided to take on the food that was being served in the cafeteria, I think you stepped out of your area of expertise. I should have seen that from the beginning, but your argument about the food was very compelling."

Miss Hodges didn't know what to say. She wasn't sure where the principal was going with this.

But Ricky felt sure. To him, it looked as though his mom was off the hook. And Miss Hodges was going to get fired!

The principal sighed again. "Miss Hodges, a lot of parents are very upset with you. My phone has been ringing off the hook since this incident happened. So as much as I hate to do this, I'm afraid I'm going to have to—"

The door burst open. "STOP!" Corey yelled. Hannah and Ben were right behind him.

The principal stood up. "What in the world are you *doing*? Have we gotten to the point where the principal of this school can't hold a private meeting without students barging in?"

Hannah stepped forward. "We're really sorry, Principal Inverno, but Club CSI has important information about this case that you need to hear before you make any decisions about what you're going to do."

Ricky jumped to his feet. "Don't listen to them! They're crazy!" He pointed at Corey. "He stole my hat!"

"How could I steal your hat?" Corey countered. "You're *wearing* your hat!"

"Only because I chased you down the hall and got it back," Ricky retorted.

Principal Inverno spoke firmly in his best principal's voice. "Everyone be quiet!" They all stopped talking. "I'm away for a few days, and this is what happens? Students stealing hats? Running through the halls? Interrupting meetings?"

Ricky sat down. Corey, Hannah, and Ben stood there quietly, looking at the floor and waiting to hear what the principal would say. Was he about to

kick them out and fire Miss Hodges? That would be terrible!

"All right," the principal said, sitting back down. "Let me share with you what I'm thinking. On the one hand, this business of barging in and interrupting meetings has got to stop. I'm happy to talk to students, but I have a schedule to follow, so you've got to make appointments if you want to talk to me. Or at least knock before you come in."

"Okay," Ben said.

"Sorry about that," Corey added.

"On the other hand," the principal continued, "I'm impressed that you've worked on investigating this problem. Miss Hodges clearly has a way with her students, which makes me really want to put an end to this meat loaf nonsense and get back to what's important: education! But the matter with the meat loaf must be addressed. . . ." The principal seemed to be thinking aloud. "And, of course, I'd like to have all the available information before I make a decision."

He pursed his lips, thinking for a moment.

"All right, Club CSI, tell me what you've discovered. And I want the facts, not your opinions."

Ricky snorted, shaking his head with disgust. His mother shot him a stern look.

Ben spoke first. "The first important thing we learned is that Mrs. Collins prepared two batches of meatless meat loaf."

"Two batches?" the principal repeated. He looked slightly panicked. "You didn't serve it again after I went to the hospital, did you?"

"No, of course not!" Mrs. Collins said.

"Two batches on that same day," Corey explained. "It was the second batch that made you and the swim team sick."

"And Dirk Brown," Hannah added.

"Right, and Dirk Brown," Corey concurred.

The principal shook his head. "I should never have had that second helping. But it was delicious. Go on."

"Based on my research on food poisoning," Hannah continued, "and what we'd heard about the symptoms of the people who got sick, we decided that the meat loaf had somehow been contaminated with *Salmonella*."

The principal nodded. "That's what my doctor said it was too. Great job researching! I'm impressed."

Hannah smiled, pleased.

"The question then was, where had the *Salmonella* come from?" Ben said. "We checked the cafeteria's kitchen, but everything seemed clean and organized, so cross-contamination there seemed highly unlikely."

"Of course it did," Mrs. Collins said gruffly. "I keep a very clean kitchen."

"At home, too," Ricky said. "She cleans the kitchen like someone's going to do surgery in there."

"We decided that one of the ingredients must have been contaminated with the bacteria," Ben went on. "And the most likely candidate for bacterial contamination was the tofu."

"Tofu?" the principal said. He turned to Miss Hodges. "Your recipe had tofu in it?" She nodded. "Huh," he said. "I didn't think I liked tofu."

"Neither did I," Corey said. "I mean, I didn't think I liked it. Not that I didn't think you liked it. I didn't know if you liked it or not."

Corey noticed his fellow investigators looking at him. "I'll just be quiet now," he said sheepishly.

"So we went to the store where Mrs. Collins bought the tofu," Ben continued.

"How did you know where she bought it?" the principal asked.

"When we checked the kitchen, we took a picture of the grocery receipt," Hannah explained. Miss Hodges smiled. Even though her job still seemed to be in jeopardy, she couldn't help but be proud of her students. Taking pictures had been good thinking on their part.

"The receipt was from Stan's, but the tofu seemed to have been handled correctly there," Ben said. "Contamination seemed unlikely."

"But then we found out that Mrs. Collins had needed more tofu, so she went to the new health food store," Corey said. He turned to Mrs. Collins. "Right?"

She nodded. "Yes, they didn't have enough tofu at Stan's to make meatless meat loaf for all the students."

"And that's where we made our biggest discovery," Hannah said proudly. "It turns out that a new employee there completely mishandled the bulk tofu."

"He didn't wash his hands after handling meat," Ben said.

"And he let the tofu sit out to get warm before Mrs. Collins picked it up," Corey piped up.

The adults all reacted to this news. So the tofu *had* been bad! That's why people got sick!

"So you see?" Hannah concluded. "The attack of the meat loaf wasn't Miss Hodges's fault at all. And it wasn't Mrs. Collins's fault either. It was the health food store employee's fault!"

The principal was impressed. He stood up to shake the hands of the three young investigators. "All right!" he said. "Mystery solved! I'm very happy to hear that none of our staff members here at Woodlands Junior High School is to blame for this incident."

"But the mystery isn't solved," Mrs. Collins said firmly. "Their explanation has big holes in it."

Everyone looked confused. Except for Miss Hodges, who nodded wearily with agreement.

"I'm afraid she's right," she said.

Chapter 16

W hat do you mean 'big holes'?" the principal asked, sitting back down.

"I used the bulk tofu from the health food store in both batches," Mrs. Collins said. "And, anyway, I baked it in the meat loaf."

"Baked it?" Ben asked.

Miss Hodges explained. "The recipe calls for baking the meat loaf in a three-hundred-and-fifty-degree oven for one hour. The cooking at a high temperature would kill any *Salmonella* in the tofu."

Everyone was baffled. Miss Hodges turned to Mrs. Collins. "Did you follow the recipe exactly?"

Mrs. Collins looked insulted. "Of course I did. The first time I make something from a new recipe, I always follow the instructions to the letter. Then the second time I make it, I improve it."

"Something tells me with this recipe, there'll be no second time," Ricky muttered.

No one was sure what to say. If the hot oven killed the bacteria, what made the principal and the swim team and Dirk Brown sick?

Ben got an idea. "Hannah," he asked, "do you have your phone with you?"

"Of course she does," Corey answered. "You might as well ask if she's got her head attached to her body."

Hannah ignored Corey's comment. "Yeah, I've got it. Why?"

"May I see the pictures of the cafeteria's kitchen, please?"

Hannah brought up the pictures she'd taken in the cafeteria's kitchen and then handed her phone to Ben. He scrolled through the photos until he found one of the recipes. Then he zoomed in until he could read the recipe.

"'Bake in a three-hundred-and-fifty-degree oven for one hour,'" he read.

"Yes, and that's exactly what I did," Mrs. Collins said. "I told you."

Ben looked up from the phone. "But the recipe doesn't say anything about making gravy. Didn't the meat loaf come with gravy?"

Miss Hodges raised her eyebrows. "That's right. You did serve the meat loaf with gravy. My recipe didn't include gravy."

Mrs. Collins looked uncomfortable. "Meat loaf needs gravy. Especially meatless meat loaf. I was sure it would be dry without it. Even if it wasn't my recipe, I wanted it to taste good. I have a reputation to maintain."

"So just to be clear, the gravy was your idea," Principal Inverno stated.

Mrs. Collins nodded grudgingly.

"Did you happen to use tofu in the gravy?" Miss Hodges asked.

Mrs. Collins looked a little uncomfortable. "Yes," she said. "I found a recipe on the Internet. I know how to make regular gravy, of course, but it's not vegetarian. I wanted to make vegetarian gravy, so I looked online. As it turns out, tofu is often used in sauces and dressings."

Miss Hodges was surprised. She'd knew that Mrs. Collins was completely against the idea of the meatless meat loaf, and yet she'd gone to some trouble to improve the recipe—with a vegetarian addition. She couldn't help but be impressed.

"From what I read about *Salmonella*, you'd have to boil the gravy to kill the bacteria," recalled Hannah.

A look of doubt passed over Mrs. Collins's face. It was quick, but Ben caught it.

"Mrs. Collins, would you mind showing us how you made the gravy?" he asked.

Club CSI, Ricky, and Principal Inverno stood in the kitchen, watching Mrs. Collins tying her apron. Miss Hodges hurried in carrying a small bag. "I got the tofu," she said.

She set the bag on the counter. Mrs. Collins took the tofu out of the bag and then set it in the refrigerator.

She turned back to the group of people watching her. "I don't like having all these people in my kitchen while I'm cooking. And students are not allowed in here," she complained.

"I understand that this is highly irregular, Mrs. Collins," Principal Inverno said sympathetically.

"But if you'll just indulge us, then we can put this whole meat loaf mess behind us."

Mrs. Collins sighed. She stood up straight and started to gather the ingredients she'd need to make the gravy. Flour, seasonings, vegetable oil . . .

Ricky complained, "I don't really get the point of this. So my mom made gravy. So what?"

The others ignored him as they watched Mrs. Collins pull a large pan out of a storage cabinet. She combined ingredients in a bowl and then turned on the stove.

As she heated the ingredients in the pan, everyone watched carefully. She added the tofu and used a whisk to make the gravy smooth as it heated up.

Soon the gravy was bubbling.

"I'm no chef, but don't those bubbles mean the gravy's boiling?" Corey asked.

Miss Hodges nodded, frowning. If Mrs. Collins brought the gravy to a boil, she would have killed the *Salmonella*.

"And that's how I made the gravy," Mrs. Collins said, smiling a little satisfied smile.

"You're sure you brought the gravy to a boil?" the principal asked.

"Positive," Mrs. Collins said. "Now that I've done it again, I even remember the look of the bubbles."

It seemed as though Club CSI's investigation of the meat loaf mystery had come to another screeching halt.

Then something occurred to Corey. "Both times?"

"What?" Mrs. Collins asked, confused.

"Did you boil the gravy both times?" he asked. "Remember? You made two batches. Didn't you have to make more gravy for the second batch?"

"Yes," Mrs. Collins said slowly, looking away.

Ben thought of something. "And the first time you told us you had to make a second batch of meat loaf for the swim team, didn't you say you had to quickly make a second batch?"

Mrs. Collins's eyes darted around. "I don't remember. I don't think so."

Hannah said, "Maybe they rushed you. You were in a big hurry, so you didn't bring the second batch of gravy all the way to a boil."

"No!" Mrs. Collins protested. "That's not right! I am always careful with my cooking!"

"Then what happened, Mrs. Collins?" the principal

asked quietly. "It seems like you need to tell us something. . . ."

Mrs. Collins thought a moment. She let out a big breath. "All right. Maybe you're right. Maybe I made those people sick. But you won't have to fire me. I'll resign."

"Mom!" Ricky cried. "No! You can't resign." He stepped closer to his mom. "It's okay. Tell them the truth."

His mom looked sternly back at him. "I already did! I told them the truth!"

"No, you didn't," Ricky said. He turned back to the principal, Miss Hodges, and Club CSI. "I made the second batch of gravy."

"Ricky, don't," his mother pleaded. "You'll get in trouble!"

"Wait a minute," Corey said. "You can cook? You? Ricky?"

Ricky nodded. "Of course I can. It's no big deal. My mom taught me."

"So you made the second batch of gravy?" Hannah asked. "The one that made people sick?"

"Yeah," Ricky admitted. "But I didn't know it was the gravy that did it until just now."

He fiddled with the strings on his hooded sweatshirt. "I came down at the end of lunch period to help my mom clean up, like I do lots of times. But she was still cooking. She said the swim team was going to eat late, so she had to make more of the meat loaf. I said I'd help, and she said I could make the gravy."

His mom touched his arm.

"I didn't know it had to boil," he said. "It didn't have any meat in it. I thought it just had to warm up. I thought you could eat tofu raw."

"You can," Hannah said. "But not if it's been contaminated. Tofu's never completely raw. There's some cooking in the process of making it. It's just that it's too easy for bulk tofu in water to end up with bacteria on it."

"And for people who eat it to end up with bacteria in them," Corey said.

The principal frowned at him. He didn't want to be reminded. He'd had a rough few days. "Sorry," Corey apologized.

Ricky faced the principal. "I'm sorry I made you sick, Principal Inverno. I didn't do it on purpose, I swear."

Principal Inverno thought for a minute, then nodded. "No, I know you didn't. In fact, you were just trying to help your mom out when she was busy. And that's very admirable."

Mrs. Collins looked hopeful. "So he's not in trouble?"

The principal shook his head. "No, he's not in trouble."

Ricky and Mrs. Collins smiled.

"But," the principal added, "he shouldn't be helping you out in the kitchen without anyone knowing about it. If you need help, we can talk about getting you some. But Ricky is a student here, not an employee."

"So the whole disaster wasn't Miss Hodges's fault at all," Hannah said. She just wanted to make sure everyone was clear about this. She liked her new forensic science teacher, and she didn't want her to be in trouble, either.

"No, it wasn't," Principal Inverno agreed. He turned toward Miss Hodges. "The problem was with the gravy, and your recipe didn't even include gravy."

"Gravy's a good idea, though," Miss Hodges said,

moving to stand next to Mrs. Collins. "As long as you boil it." She smiled.

"I'm impressed with the job your students did investigating this situation," the principal said. "You've obviously inspired them. I think you must be doing a good job of teaching forensic science. Did you help them with their investigation?"

Miss Hodges smiled at Club CSI. "Nope," she said. "They did it all on their own."

"Yay, us!" Corey said.

"Well, now that that's settled, I think we all need to get to class or to work," Principal Inverno announced.

He started toward the door.

"Principal Inverno?" Ben said, raising his hand.

"Yes, Ben?"

"There's just one more thing. . . ."

Chapter 17

Jack stared at the stack of papers on the little beat-up desk in his crowded office at Stan's. Bills. Invoices. Letters from the bank.

He thought about his grandfather working in this same office, back when Stan's was the only place to buy groceries for miles around. There were plenty of customers back then. But not now. Every week it seemed as though fewer customers came into the small neighborhood grocery store. How much longer could they hold on?

There was a knock on the door. "Come in," Jack said.

His cashier, Roberta, stuck her head in. "There are some kids here to see you."

"Kids?" he said. "I hope they're not looking for a contribution or something."

"I don't think so," she said. "They're the same ones that were here the other day asking about tofu."

Jack clenched his jaw and then smiled. "Oh, right. I remember them. Tell 'em to come on in, if they can all squeeze into my palatial office."

Roberta pulled her head back out of the doorway. Jack stood up and faced the door.

Hannah, Corey, and Ben came in and said hi. Jack greeted them warmly.

"What can I do for you? Do you need more information on tofu?"

He gave them a big smile. Hannah shook her head.

"No," she said. "We just thought we'd let you know how our investigation came out."

Jack looked puzzled. "Investigation? Oh, that's right. That's what your club is all about—CSI."

"Right," Corey said. "After you told us you sent Mrs. Collins over to the new health food store for more tofu, we went over there and talked to the owners."

"They seem like a nice couple," Jack said pleasantly.

"Oh, they are," Ben agreed. "Maybe too nice."

"Too nice?" Jack asked. "I didn't think it was

possible to be too nice in this business. The customers really appreciate it."

"The customers like it," Corey said. "But sometimes when you're too nice, you make mistakes hiring employees."

Jack's left eye twitched. Just a little. But Ben noticed it.

"I see what you mean," Jack said. "But we've all made mistakes hiring people. That's just part of running a business. If you go into business when you grow up, you'll find that out for yourselves."

He sat down in his chair and then turned back to the paperwork on his desk.

"Well," he said, "I'm sorry to hear they hired someone incompetent at the health food store. They really should be more careful. Thanks for coming back to let me know that's where the bad tofu came from."

"Actually," Ben said, "we didn't say anything about bad tofu coming from an incompetent employee."

Jack shrugged. "Well, that's what you were implying."

Ben nodded. "You're right. It was a bad employee

who sold Mrs. Collins the contaminated tofu. His name's Jim."

Jack looked a little impatient. "Okay, kids. That's great. Now, if you'll excuse me . . ."

"Jim looked really familiar to me when we met him," Ben said. "But I couldn't figure out where I knew him from."

Jack sat very still.

"I thought about it for quite a while, trying to remember where I'd met him before," Ben continued. "Then it came to me: I'd never met him before."

Jack smiled a tight smile. "I guess we all make mistakes."

"It wasn't that I'd met him," Ben said. "It was that he reminded me of someone. Not just the way he looked. The way he talked and moved too."

Ben paused. "He reminded me of you."

Jack took a deep breath through his nose.

"Because he's your brother," Ben continued.

Corey pointed at the old family photo on the wall. "That's him right there, when you two were kids. He grew up, but the bones in his face didn't change completely. You can tell it's Jim."

"You said he moved away, but he didn't," Hannah

said. "He stayed here in town."

"And you sent him to work at the new health food store, because it was ruining your business," Ben said. "You wanted him to sabotage their reputation."

Jack stood up again. He didn't look friendly anymore. He looked angry. "Now look . . . ," he said in a low, threatening voice.

But as he took a step forward, Principal Inverno crowded into the office. "Okay, we'll take it from here, kids. Good job."

Ben, Hannah, and Corey stepped just outside the office, so there was room for a police officer to come in.

"The police?" Jack said in disbelief. "You've got the police in on this?"

"Yup," Corey said. "Once they heard what your brother, Jim, had to say about your plan to ruin the health food store, they were real eager to meet you."

"Besides," added Principal Inverno, "you're not the only one with a brother." He turned to the police officer. "Go ahead, bro. Do your job."

After school that day, Club CSI met in the science lab at school. "I'd say our first case was a huge success," Corey announced.

"I agree," Hannah said.

"Second the motion," Ben said, laughing.

Miss Hodges stuck her head out of the small room off the lab that she used as her office. "Need anything, Club CSI?"

"No, thank you, Faculty Advisor," Hannah said, smiling.

"Actually," Corey said, snapping his fingers, "can you bring us some snacks next time?"

"Corey!" Ben and Hannah said at the same time.

But Miss Hodges didn't mind. "I'd be happy to. I can make some tofu chocolate-chip cookies!" she said with a wink.

Everyone laughed, and Miss Hodges grinned at her students. "On a serious note, I'm tremendously grateful for your help in clearing my name. So thank you. Okay, carry on."

She went back into her office and then closed the door.

"You know," Corey said, "word's spread through the whole school about how we investigated the meat loaf attack and how we figured out who did it and how our investigation even led to a couple of arrests."

"I know," Hannah said. "I've heard people talking about it. And pointing at us."

"We're famous!" Corey said. "And I always thought I'd be famous for my basketball skills!"

"I've had a bunch of people come up to me, asking if they can join the club," Ben said. "What do you think?"

"I think that means we are definitely not a geek club!" Hannah said with a smile.

"Totally," Corey added. "And now, if you'll excuse me, I've got basketball practice." He grabbed his backpack and headed for the door. "See you tomorrow."

"See you," Ben said. "Have a good practice."

But Hannah didn't say anything. She seemed to be lost in thought.

"Um, hello? Hannah? See you tomorrow?" Corey said.

"Oh," she said. "Right. See you tomorrow."

"What were you thinking about?" Corey asked.

"I was thinking about how I can hardly wait," she confessed.

"Until what?" Ben asked.

"Our next case!"

David **Lewman** never ate meat loaf from the school cafeteria, but he took his mother's meat loaf sandwiches to school lots of times, and they were delicious! David has written more than sixty-five books starring SpongeBob SquarePants, Jimmy Neutron, the Fairly OddParents, G.I. Joe, the Wild Thornberrys, and other popular characters. He has also written scripts for many acclaimed television shows. David lives in Los Angeles with his wife, Donna, and their dog, Pirkle.

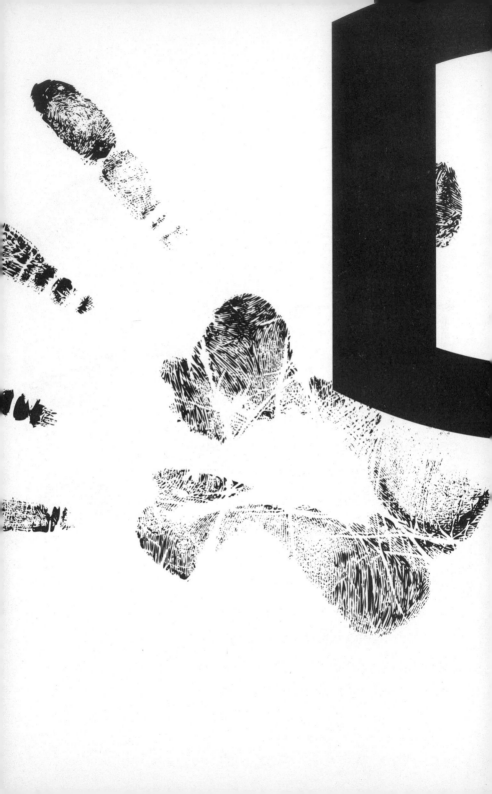